# DWEEB

# OTHER YEARLING BOOKS
# YOU WILL ENJOY

## *A Dog Called Grk*
Joshua Doder

## *I Put a Spell on You*
Adam Selzer

## *Mudshark*
Gary Paulsen

## *Brendan Buckley's Universe and Everything In It*
Sundee T. Frazier

## *Wild River*
P. J. Petersen

# DWEEB

## BURGERS, BEASTS, AND BRAINWASHED BULLIES

### Aaron Starmer

A YEARLING BOOK

Text copyright © 2009 by Aaron Starmer
Illustrations copyright © 2009 by Andy Rash

All rights reserved. Published in the United States by Yearling, an imprint of Random House Children's Books, a division of Random House, Inc., New York. Originally published in hardcover in the United States by Delacorte Press, an imprint of Random House Children's Books, a division of Random House, Inc., New York, in 2009.

Yearling and the jumping horse design are registered trademarks of Random House, Inc.

Visit us on the Web! www.randomhouse.com/kids

Educators and librarians, for a variety of teaching tools, visit us at
www.randomhouse.com/teachers

The Library of Congress has cataloged the hardcover edition of this work as follows:
Starmer, Aaron.
Dweeb : burgers, beasts, and brainwashed bullies / Aaron Starmer.
p. cm.
Summary: After being framed for stealing bake sale money, the five smartest boys in eighth grade are imprisoned in a small room beneath their junior high school in Ho-Ho-Kus, New Jersey, and must use their nerdish powers to expose a conspiracy involving fast food, standardized testing, and a school full of overachieving zombies.
ISBN 978-0-385-73705-0 (hc) — ISBN 978-0-385-90643-2 (glb) —
ISBN 978-0-375-89344-5 (ebook)
[1. Junior high schools—Fiction. 2. Schools—Fiction. 3. Conspiracies—Fiction.] I. Title.
PZ7.S7972Dw 2009
[Fic]—dc22
2009000500

ISBN 978-0-375-84605-2 (pbk.)

Printed in the United States of America
10 9 8 7 6 5 4 3 2

First Yearling Edition

Random House Children's Books supports the First Amendment
and celebrates the right to read.

For Cate

# Prologue

**E**verything was normal. Everything was average. It was a typical April morning in Ho-Ho-Kus, New Jersey.

Vice Principal Snodgrass had arrived early at school, before even the janitors. Sitting in his office, he separated an immense mound of cash into five equal piles. Then he placed them all in a duffel bag, which he hid in the shadows beneath his desk.

He lifted the receiver of his phone and dialed a number. It cycled through a few rings, then transferred to an unnamed voice-mail box.

"It's early, I know," Snodgrass said. "But everything is

in place. I'll have the evidence soon enough. I just thought I'd give you an update. Thank you . . . thank you for the opportunity, sir."

He placed the receiver back in its cradle. Almost as soon as he did, it started to ring. He waited a moment, so as not to seem overly anxious. Then he put it to his ear and cringed as a familiar voice asked, "Are you ready?"

"Of course I'm ready," Snodgrass responded. "Don't worry. It's already begun."

He slammed the phone down. Then he lifted a sheet of paper from his desk. On it was a list of five names:

DENTON KENSINGTON
WENDELL SCOOP
EDDIE GREEN
ELIJAH ROSEN
BIJAY BHARATA

He slipped the list into a folder, and he placed the folder in his desk drawer. Then he rapped his bloated knuckles nervously against the wood and looked out the window to see the sun introducing itself on the horizon and illuminating the damp soccer fields.

A muffled grunt and growl broke him out of his daze. He rose and walked over to his closet. He opened the door.

"Easy, boy," Snodgrass whispered. "You've already had a drink this morning. We just have to move you. So don't you dare try to bite me again."

He paused and looked down at the curled-up shape in

the dark corner of the closet. The growl was now a low, steady rumble.

"It works. Just look at you. And what we've done . . . it's incredible, you know," Snodgrass whispered. "If only you had the ability to understand that. Everyone else soon will. . . ."

# Chapter 1
## DENTON

Denton Kensington sat at the breakfast table, sipping tomato juice. With a sharp flick of his wrist, he straightened up the *Financial Times* and had a look at the date.

Friday, April 12.

He had been in America for not even eight months. It seemed so much longer.

As he unfolded the paper, his mother came up behind him and hugged him around the shoulders.

"I'm so proud of you, dear." She smothered his forehead with a kiss. "Both your father and I are so proud."

Denton pulled away. "Argh, Mum, you'll wrinkle my shirt. I just pressed it."

"And it looks lovely, dear. You look lovely."

"In America, looking lovely isn't exactly cool," Denton explained. "As a matter of fact, I don't think it's cool anywhere."

"Well, maybe it should be." His mother smiled. "Looking lovely will get you a good job and a good girl. Who wouldn't want that?"

"Well, I don't happen to have either," Denton told her.

"That's because you're only thirteen, dear."

"Don't remind me," Denton grumbled.

Back in England, there were other kids like Denton— prim, proper, and concerned with world affairs and correct grammar. He used to at least chat with those kids in school, sometimes share a chuckle or two. On occasion, he had even invited them over to his house to watch old movies on the couch or build model sailboats in his father's study.

That had all ended when his father got a banking job in New York City, bought a house in some strange little town called Ho-Ho-Kus, New Jersey, and moved the family overseas. Eighth grade, as it was called in America, soon followed.

Eighth grade was full of far too many swaggering, boorish boys and chatterbox girls. While they had plenty of those in England too, it wasn't all of them. It might not have been all of them in New Jersey either, but to Denton it certainly seemed like it.

His new school was enormous. There were four hundred kids in the eighth grade alone. To find five or six he could connect with seemed an awfully big task. After months of empty searches, he stopped looking for friends. Time was better spent studying, getting ready for university. Cambridge or Oxford—those were the only ones worth attending, in Denton's mind. And if he was going to get into either, if he was going to find his way back to his beloved England, he had to focus on his future.

"How old would you rather be?" Denton's mother asked him.

Denton thought it over for a moment. "Forty-seven," he finally said.

"Forty-seven?" His mother laughed. "That's a peculiar age to pick."

"At forty-seven, I'd have a good retirement plan already established," Denton explained. "Perhaps I'd be able to afford a Bentley. I could be a barrister. That certainly beats eighth grade."

"Don't be so sure about that," his mother said, fixing the part in his hair with her long, elegant fingers. "Thirteen is a grand age. And I think you'll find today will be a grand day. Your best in America. Maybe your best ever."

Denton looked up at her with more than a little suspicion. "I wouldn't count on that," he said.

He turned to the kitchen window and looked out into morning. Instead of his quaint English hometown of Ruttle-on-Tillsbury, where his family once had a garden with immaculate hedgerows, tulips, and fountains, he was treated to the images of suburban Ho-Ho-Kus: his neighbors' stinky little pug and their rickety old trampoline.

He hated pugs (too slobbery!). He hated trampolines

(too dangerous!). He hated Ho-Ho-Kus (too . . . too . . . New Jersey!). But this was his life.

School that day started no grander than any other day.

"Well, well, well. If it isn't Harry Snotter, the ol' Duke of Dork," Tyler Kelly said in homeroom. He finished the sentiment with a knuckle punch to Denton's arm.

"Blimey!" Denton howled. "What was that for?"

"I don't know." Tyler shrugged. " 'Cause you say stupid stuff like 'blimey.' "

"But I said it *after* you punched me," Denton pleaded.

"I can predict the future," Tyler said. Then he punched him another time.

"Blimey!"

"See," Tyler said. "I knew you'd say it again. Just keepin' you honest, Frodo." Tyler raised his fist once more and swung it down. Denton flinched. But Tyler's fist stopped short, about two inches from Denton's arm.

"You're lucky," Tyler said. "You wouldn't have said it this time. You were going to say 'Crikey!' or something like that." He cackled loudly to himself, then turned and walked away, leaving Denton to rub his bruised arm.

Denton's first class of the day was social studies, where he was to give a presentation on Bangladesh. He took his place at the front of the classroom and launched into it almost as soon as the other kids had reached their seats. And while Denton's teacher was absolutely charmed by his masterful distillation of facts, by his commentary on agriculture and population density and religion and just about everything you could say about a country half a world away, his fellow students were less than enthusiastic.

Surely the girls will be impressed by my knowledge, Denton had thought. But even the girls who used to peer coyly over their books at Denton when he first came to school were now thoroughly uninterested. They sent texts under their desks. Or they drew inky temporary tattoos on the skin of their hands. Some just stared at the walls, their faces tired and blank.

After he finished, he bowed and received absolutely no applause. Then he took a seat at his desk. At that moment, he felt truly like a *foreigner,* for lack of a better word.

And his next class was gym. And gym was even worse.

Denton wasn't opposed to sports. In England he had played cricket and water polo and even a bit of rugby. But physical education in America was nowhere near as civilized as all that. It was organized chaos—all obstacle courses and foam balls and greasy mesh pinnies. Not to mention the fact that Coach McKenzie was a tyrant. He was constantly pointing his meaty finger at Denton, commanding him to shinny up ropes, to run wind sprints, to serve as a crash-test dummy for the more muscular boys to throw to the mats during wrestling demonstrations.

Lacing up his sneakers in the locker room, Denton felt a tap on his shoulder. He hesitated to turn around. He had fallen victim to too many sneak attacks over the years.

"Peter Pan!" came the thundering voice of Coach McKenzie. "My office. Now!"

Denton turned and looked up to see McKenzie stomping away. Reluctantly, he followed.

McKenzie's office was like a small apartment. There was a desk and a dresser with a small television on it. In the corner was a small cot, presumably for midday naps. There were framed letters from former students on the wall, and certificates from various civic organizations. One wall was completely covered with a map of the world. There were green thumbtacks all over it—Australia, Kenya, Brazil, even his home of England. Denton also noticed two red thumbtacks. They were stuck in the center of Louisiana and on the top border of South Korea.

"No gym class for you today," McKenzie barked.

"Really? Why?" Denton turned away from the map and faced McKenzie, not bothering to conceal his joy.

"Vice Principal Snodgrass wants to see you. ASAP. Which means I want you outta my sight and in his office in the next five minutes."

"Yes, sir."

"Git 'er done," Coach McKenzie said, slapping Denton on the back a little too hard.

Denton had never met Vice Principal Snodgrass, but it was common knowledge that he handed out detention as if it were a vaccine. He figured everyone could use a good dose. Denton didn't deserve detention, though. He had done nothing wrong.

The Idaho Tests, that must be it, he thought. The most important tests of junior high, they were taking place next Friday. They covered all the bases—math, science, English, social studies. Everyone from fifth to eighth grade had to take them, but for eighth graders, they were of monumental importance. Not only did they determine what classes you were allowed to take in high school, they also gauged where your junior high ranked in relation to all the other junior highs in the country.

Teachers were taking the tests very seriously. Denton was taking them very seriously. Undoubtedly, Snodgrass was too. After all, he had scheduled a pep rally for the day before the test. And now he probably just wanted to check with the best students to make sure everything was going well. Which it was. Denton had been quizzing himself every night, memorizing historical facts and figures. He had been hard at work, programming his brain. Tests weren't like his social life. Tests he could handle.

Relaxed, Denton opened the door to the vice principal's office and saw that it was empty. A line of five chairs sat in front of Snodgrass's desk. Denton used his fingers to straighten the part in his wavy brown hair. Then he sat down, crossed his legs, and waited.

# Chapter 2
# WENDELL

"Do you play basketball?" Sally Dibbs asked Wendell Scoop at the bus stop.

"No," Wendell replied quickly.

It was a question he heard a lot, and it always irritated him. He knew she wasn't asking just because he was black. It was because he was only thirteen and he was already six foot six—six foot nine if he counted his hair, a spiky, messy lump that stuck out in all directions like an old toothbrush. He weighed in at an impressive 240 pounds, which meant he also heard the next question a lot.

"Do you play football?"

"No."

"Oh . . ."

Sally nibbled at her thumbnail and looked up at the clouds. "Baseball?" she asked tentatively.

"No!" Wendell barked back. Sometimes he thought about how great it would be to lose a hundred pounds and have his legs chopped off at the knees in some heroic accident. Then he would never have to answer such pointless questions again.

"What do you play, then?" Sally asked.

He was tempted to yell "Nothing!" as he often did in these situations. Sally was new in town, though, and she probably didn't know any better.

"Video games," he finally answered.

He could not have given a truer answer. When it came to video games, Wendell was an all-star—the LeBron James of Halo, the Peyton Manning of Warcraft. He had heard that in Japan and South Korea there were professional computer-game players who were treated like rock stars. They signed autographs. They were on TV. They got girls. Girls! For playing computer games! It seemed too unbelievable, but he often thought it was his destiny.

"As long as I keep playing," he would tell his mother, "I'll end up rich and famous in the end."

"Just do what you love, babe," she'd say. "That's all your daddy and I ask."

Wendell knew deep down she hoped he would become a software engineer, a computer programmer. After all, as good as he was at video games, Wendell was even better at math. Over the years, trophies from Math Olympiads piled up in his cluttered bedroom, competing for face time with anime posters and action figures.

Numbers were more than just symbols to him, more than things to be added and divided and jumbled together in equations. They were paths to solutions. They made life (some of it, at least) clear, definite, controllable.

Wendell's older brother, Trent, was also a math whiz. He was a sophomore at MIT, where he was acing all his classes. He was smart and happy and he was Wendell's hero. When Trent was thirteen, he was big and goofy too. By the time he entered college, he had come into his own.

People said it was more a boost in confidence than anything—walking with a stiffer posture, talking with a stronger voice. Though Wendell attributed it to something else: Trent had a girlfriend. Her name was Keisha and she was beautiful, with glowing eyes and a contagious laugh. They had been dating for nearly two years, which ruled out the possibility that she was dating him on a dare. As impossible as it seemed, she liked Trent—loved him, even.

"How did you do it?" Wendell asked his brother the day before eighth grade started.

"What's that?"

"Get a girl like Keisha? I mean . . . get any girl?"

Trent laughed. "Just wait, little brother. Give it time."

Four and a half years. That was a long time Wendell had to wait until college. An eternity. He filled it by playing video games, solving math problems, and writing computer code. While his old friends Carl and Ray and Dennis were playing touch football in the park, Wendell was behind the glow of his computer screen. While they were sneaking into Suzy Greenburg's sleepover party, Wendell was firing through a book of Sudoku puzzles.

The guys still said hello in the halls, and sometimes sat next to Wendell at lunch for a few minutes to pick his brain about video game cheat codes. That was it, though, and Wendell couldn't really blame them. They used to invite him along, but he always declined. After a while, they stopped inviting.

Now, Wendell sat alone on the bus, in the front seat, his long legs bent sharply and pressed against the steel barrier separating him and the bus driver. Sally Dibbs sat behind him, playing her iPod too loudly and cluelessly kicking the seat along with the beat of a Jonas Brothers song.

"Quit it!" Wendell said, standing up and turning around.

"Excuse me." Sally smiled and pulled an earbud out of one ear.

"You're kicking my seat."

"I am?" She blushed. "Sorry. I sometimes don't realize I'm doing things that . . . you know, I'm actually doing."

"Well . . . quit doing them," Wendell grumbled.

Sally twisted her mouth, which made her nose wiggle and her eyes blink. Then she smiled again, and nodded. It was odd, and awkward, and Wendell sat back down, choosing just to ignore her.

A queasy feeling overtook him as the bus bumped and swerved its way into the Ho-Ho-Kus Junior High parking lot. It happened a lot. He had a weak stomach, and it always went sour when he was nervous. School itself didn't make Wendell nervous, but on this particular morning, he had woken with three monster zits on his face—one on his left cheek, one on his chin, and one right in the middle of his nose.

Acne was becoming a constant problem for him. It began erupting on his face about two years before, at the same time he started growing like a sponge in a hurricane. He had hit puberty before everyone else, and he had hit it hard. His voice skipped the part where it cracked, and almost overnight it became a low, manly rumble. His house was littered with bent and broken chairs that had met their demise due to Wendell's new girth. Clothing had to be given away within weeks of buying it. He felt like the Incredible Expanding Boy, but that was something he usually could deal with.

Acne was different. Some mornings he would scrub his face until it hurt, but it never seemed to make a difference. His skin was the perfect soil for a crop of whiteheads, and it didn't matter that his mom said all his classmates were going through similar problems. When his face was fresh with zits, Wendell couldn't help thinking that everyone was staring at him or laughing behind cupped hands. His nerves would get the best of him. His stomach would do somersaults. There was only one cure.

It wasn't a pill or a potion. It wasn't a treatment. It was a person.

"Hi, Nurse Bloom," Wendell said, poking his head into her office. "Whatcha reading?"

Nurse Bloom sat behind her desk engrossed in a book. Wendell could see only the picture on the cover, a jumble of numbers. She held a single finger in the air, then took a pencil off her desk and jotted something in the book. Then she placed it down, looked at him, and smiled warmly.

"Just a little Sudoku," she said.

"Sweet," Wendell said. "I love Sudoku."

"Only the coolest do," she said with a wink. "No one even knew about Sudoku when I was your age. Kids like us had to get by with a Rubik's Cube."

"And an abacus?" Wendell joked cautiously.

"And an abacus," Nurse Bloom echoed with an airy laugh. "Wendell Scoop! If I didn't know you were such an awesome guy, I'd think you were calling me old."

Wendell shrugged and pursed his lips, trying not to smile.

"But of course you wouldn't do that," Nurse Bloom said, standing up. "Which leaves the question. What can I help you with, my friend? Stomach again?"

He nodded with a twinge of guilt.

"Well, mister," she said. "You know the drill. Have a rest over there. Do those breathing exercises I taught you. It'll go away before you know it."

Wendell made his way over to a small cot in the corner and eased himself down onto it, curling his large body up as the springs groaned under his weight.

"Thanks, Nurse Bloom. As always."

"No problem, Wen," she said. "Someday you'll have this stomach thing beat. Then I won't have the pleasure of your visits. Good for you. Bad for me."

"I'll still visit," Wendell said from the cot. "I'm sure some other illness will get me."

"I don't hear those breathing exercises," she gently scolded.

"Sorry, ma'am."

Wendell began taking deep breaths. There was nothing in the world he wouldn't do for Nurse Bloom. She was the kindest, most beautiful woman he had ever met. Forget movie stars. They had nothing on Nurse Bloom. She was tall, with dark eyes and dark hair that spilled over her white coat like hot fudge over ice cream. She seemed younger than most teachers in the school, but at the same time, she seemed wiser. When she walked, it was with pure confidence. Her arms and legs were hypnotically fluid. In math terms, she was a fractal—the closer you looked at her, the more perfect she appeared. Even her smallest gestures communicated a giant beauty.

There were rumors that she had actually studied to be a chemist but had decided nursing was a more noble profession. She was certainly smart. Not only did she know how to treat any ailment, she knew the answer to every trivia question Wendell could throw at her.

"Nurse Bloom?" Wendell asked between deep breaths.

"Yes?"

"Bet you don't know who invented Pong. You know, the first video game."

No more than two seconds passed and she had an answer. "Nolan Bushnell," she called out.

"You're incredible!"

"No, Wen, you're the incredible one. You ready for the Idaho Tests? I bet you rock the math one."

"I can only hope," he called back. Wendell closed his eyes, continued his breathing, and tried not to think about the Idaho Tests at all. The Idaho Tests were the definition of boredom. The math questions were easy and uninspired. Necessary or not, the tests didn't teach him a single thing.

So instead, he thought only of Nurse Bloom. He imagined what it might be like to be married to her. It was about the most exciting thing he could imagine. Pure heaven.

The ring of a phone broke Wendell out of his daze.

"Nurse's office," he heard Nurse Bloom answer. "Yes . . . yes. He's right here. No . . . no, just a stomachache . . . I don't think that should be a problem. I'll send him right over."

Wendell sat up.

"Wen?" Nurse Bloom called out. "How you doin'?"

"Better."

"That was just Vice Principal Snodgrass," she said. "If you're feeling up to it, he'd like to see you."

"Really? Why would he want to see me?"

"Beats me," she said. "But you should probably get over there soon. I think it might be important."

Wendell stood, almost banging his head on the low ceiling. "Okay," he said. "I guess . . . I guess I should go."

"You'll do fine," Nurse Bloom said, shooting him a thumbs-up as he walked past.

Loping down the hall, away from the safety of Nurse Bloom's office, Wendell wasn't so sure. He knew that kids were only called to Vice Principal Snodgrass's office if they were in trouble. Tyler Kelly, the toughest kid in school, was there constantly, and he always ended up in detention. He had even been suspended a few times.

The thing was, Tyler Kelly had a girlfriend. Actually, he had dated a lot of girls. Darla Barnes, Mary Dobski, Emma Radson—the list went on and on. Was there a correlation? None of them seemed to mind that Tyler called Wendell hurtful things like "Queen Kong" or that he was constantly pretending to faint whenever Wendell lifted his arm. No, they usually just laughed. Because good girls liked bad boys. The way of the world, as far as Wendell knew. Which made him think his brother, Trent, was probably no exception to this rule. Why else would Keisha stick around?

Wendell quickened his pace down the hall. It didn't really matter why he had been called to Snodgrass's office. If he could leave there saddled with a bad rep, then maybe it would be worth suffering a little detention. When he finally reached Snodgrass's office, he found the door open a crack. He pushed it and peered inside. Denton Kensington, the kid from England, was sitting in a chair. Four empty chairs were lined up next to him.

"Hello," Denton said with surprise. "Have a seat, I suppose."

Wendell shrugged his shoulders and then lowered himself carefully onto a chair. Luckily, it didn't break.

# Chapter 3
# EDDIE

Eddie Green woke at 6:00 a.m. on Friday, April 12. He inhaled two bowls of Frosted Flakes, chomped on two apples, and sucked down a chocolate milk shake, which constituted a relatively small breakfast for him. Then he decided to cut the grass. His parents paid him thirty dollars a week to cut it, and now was as good a time as any.

When he finished the grass, it was 6:50, and to make it to school by 7:30, he needed to leave soon. It was more than six miles from his house to Ho-Ho-Kus Junior High, and he wasn't going to bother with the bus—he was going to run the entire way. It usually took him thirty minutes.

As he packed up his backpack with last night's unfinished homework, his father grabbed him by the shoulder and turned him around.

"Hey, Chief," his father said, slapping fifty dollars into Eddie's hand. "Be good now. Mom and I are going to miss you."

It was an odd comment. Miss him? He went to school every day. He'd be home in the afternoon.

"Sure thing, Old Boy," Eddie said. "And thanks for the extra twenty."

Within ten seconds, Eddie was out the door, hoofing it south on Rivington. His father stood by the front window, sipping his coffee and waving.

Only thirteen years old and Eddie was already the best runner on the Ho-Ho-Kus High School cross-country team. Never mind the fact that he wasn't even in high school yet. A mere technicality. When word reached the coach that there was an eighth grader who could run a four-and-a-half-minute mile, he bent every rule to have Eddie run varsity. Eddie didn't disappoint him, either. At the end of the season, he qualified for the state meet. He placed ninth.

As Eddie zipped his way along the suburban streets, he fueled himself with visions of next year's meet. Six of the top ten finishers were graduating. His times were improving every day. With the morning sun warming his scalp through his blond buzz cut, Eddie had warm thoughts. Destiny was lining up for him.

When he arrived at school, he had hardly broken a sweat. Kids were congregated on the front steps, waiting for the first bell to call them to homeroom. Tyler Kelly was holding court.

"I'm gonna eat fifty Mackers Chicken Wingdings in one sitting," Tyler announced. "You can bet on that!"

Tyler shifted his gaze to watch Eddie hop up the steps. "Hey, Speedy Gonzales," he said.

Eddie stopped. "Hey there, Tyler."

"You are outta your friggin' mind, aren't you?" Tyler laughed. "Did you run all the way to school?"

"Most of the way," Eddie shot back. His mouth kept going before his brain could calculate the consequences. "I had to stop to give your mom a good-morning smooch."

"Oooooooh," howled a chorus of onlookers.

Tyler didn't do anything at first. He just nodded, taking the comment in stride. After a few seconds, he finally spoke.

"If I didn't know any better, I'd think you were looking for a beat-down. I'd give you one too, but I'd have to catch your twitchy butt first."

"That's true," Eddie agreed, jogging in place to release his excess energy. "Maybe I'll run backwards to give you a little help."

"You're a spaz, Green," Tyler said. "You'll always be a spaz. And running backwards, forwards, or sideways, I ain't gonna chase you. I'm liable to catch a deadly dose of your twitch-and-fidgets."

"Point taken," Eddie responded. Then he turned away and bounced up the stairs, relieved to have dodged a bullet. Eddie was always dodging bullets.

As he entered the school, he could hear Tyler behind him saying, "See, ladies, I can show mercy. Even to a spaz."

To his classmates, it seemed a minor taunt, something to call a guy with too much energy. Eddie knew better. His mind was as fast as his feet. It could process and contain information at a frantic pace. His head was crammed full of trivia, with vocabulary and word origins. He knew what the insults really meant. His classmates were saying there was something wrong with him, that he was broken.

Teachers told him the same thing, only they used different words. They called him a distraction and scolded him for talking before thinking, accepting wild dares, and doing stupid things just for the sake of doing them.

But no matter what classmates, teachers, or even doctors said, Eddie simply was who he was: a boy who could not be slowed down.

Second period for Eddie meant health class. Health class meant having to dam off all the lewd comments that were threatening to flow forth from his mouth. It was always a monumental task.

He tapped his foot nervously on the floor as Mrs. Larson conducted her lesson. He knew that an off-color remark would land him in the vice principal's office, so he had to make sure to deploy only grade-A material. Given just one chance, he'd have to make the best of it.

When the classroom phone rang, he took a deep breath. It was a well-needed intermission. He could whisper a joke to a classmate to blow off a little steam. Then he would recollect himself and prepare for his grand finale.

He turned to Hal Melman, who was sitting one desk over.

"Hey, Hal," he whispered. "What do you call a guy with no arms and no legs whose—"

Before he could finish his joke, Mrs. Larson cut him off.

"Mr. Green," she said, clearing her throat with an air of authority.

"Yes?"

"Snodgrass."

It was a call Eddie had grown accustomed to, but he wasn't sure why he was receiving it now. Surely it couldn't have been due to the morning incident with Tyler Kelly.

"Really?" Eddie responded. "I haven't even had a chance to say anything yet."

The class erupted in laughter. They, too, knew it was only a matter of time. Mrs. Larson simply shrugged and pointed to the door. "But no running," she said.

Eddie played it off as if it were nothing. As he leapt from his chair and did a little shuffle to the front of class, he raised his hands like a prizefighter and announced his exit.

"My work here is done," he said. "Pray for me, people. Pray for me." Applause followed him as he exited the room.

Eddie knew he was on shaky ground. His grades were great. He was dedicated to his running. He just couldn't stay out of detention.

It hadn't been a big deal when he was younger. But ever since Snodgrass had entered the picture, punishment had become more and more frequent.

Snodgrass had arrived at school last year. Eddie remembered the vice principal's first day well. It had started with an assembly, where Snodgrass stood in front of the entire school and announced, "I'll turn you all into Renaissance children."

"What's a rent-a-cop child?" someone yelled out from the dark auditorium.

"A Renaissance child . . . well, it's only just a perfect kid . . . in every way," Snodgrass said smoothly.

"Does that require a lot of studying?" someone else shouted.

Snodgrass chuckled. He shrugged his shoulders, as if to say: "What do you think, buddy?"

Had Snodgrass been granted absolute power, he would have suspended Eddie by now. Suspension from school equaled suspension from the cross-country team. Eddie's one saving grace was Principal Phipps.

Whenever Eddie got in trouble, Phipps saw to it that the punishment was light. Though he had spoken to Eddie's father the last time he'd come to pick Eddie up from detention.

Pressing his ear against the door to Phipps's office, Eddie heard his father ask, "Do you think he needs more discipline?"

"Discipline is great," Phipps had said, "but school should be about forming unique and vibrant individuals. Your son's an individual, Mr. Green. He's never hurt anybody or caused mischief out of malice. He's just a boy with too much boy in him."

As Eddie's father drove him home that afternoon, he said, "Every school could use a Principal Phipps."

"Got that right, Old Boy," Eddie responded, grateful that the principal had let him off easy—and appreciated his sense of humor.

The year before, Eddie had accepted a dare to run around the school in the dead of winter wearing nothing but his underwear. He was eventually apprehended by a dumbfounded janitor, who tossed a blanket around him and shepherded him to Phipps's office. When Phipps asked him how his feet didn't freeze in the four inches of snow, Eddie poked his toes out from beneath the blanket and revealed the frayed remains of his underwear.

"If you tear them in half, they make darn good moccasins," Eddie stated.

Phipps couldn't help smiling. "Do us all a favor," he said. "Sign up for home ec classes next year—your fashion instincts need some refinement. And thinking things over, taking things slow . . . it's not as boring as you might think."

They want me to go slower, Eddie thought. I'll give them slow. As he made his way to Snodgrass's office Friday morning, he dragged his feet, ran his hand across lockers, and zagged like a stunt plane through the halls.

Slow for Eddie was still quick for most. Before long, he was at Snodgrass's office.

He let himself in, as he often did. But instead of

Snodgrass, there were two other students sitting there: Wendell Scoop, a computer nerd, and Denton Kensington, a British lord or something ridiculous like that.

"Top of the morning," Eddie said with a wink. "This is where you try out for *American Idol*, right?"

# Chapter 4
## ELIJAH

Behind the backstop, in a dark corner of the playground, there was a small patch of concrete, an inconsequential spill left over from the construction of the foursquare court. Checking over both shoulders, Elijah Rosen removed a can of black spray paint from his tattered backpack, uncapped it, and carefully unleashed the dark pigment on the sad little patch. He wrote two letters: *e.r.* Not quite satisfied, he finished off his graffiti with a capital *A* in a haphazard circle, the international sign for anarchy.

Elijah was pretty sure he was an anarchist. As far as he knew, anarchists were people who didn't follow rules, who marched, as they said, to the beat of their own drummer. Ever since a short story he had written titled "The Stairway to Despair" had won a prize from the Northern New Jersey Council for the Arts, Elijah fit that bill. He had decided he wasn't like the other kids at Ho-Ho-Kus Junior High. He was an artist.

When he was younger, people called him Eli. Elijah declared an end to those days; he was now Elijah and Elijah only. The khaki pants and polo shirts his parents had picked out for him over the years were sent directly to Goodwill. In their place, he wore thrift-store clothes more befitting a great writer. This included a bomber jacket and dark blue, strategically torn jeans. His eyes worked well enough, but he bought a pair of black-framed glasses, popped clear lenses in them, and wore them constantly. His hair was no longer combed and parted. It was a carefully maintained rat's nest—dark, tangled, and droopy.

That was exactly how his sister, Tara, described his writing—dark, tangled, and droopy.

"Well, that's how the world is," Elijah told her. "Dark, tangled, and . . . well, it's dark and tangled, at least."

On the first day of eighth grade, Tyler Kelly commented on Elijah's new look.

"Hey, Eli! You trying out for *High School Musical*?" he asked. "I heard they were looking for new chicks."

"Hilarious, Tyler," Elijah said with a roll of the eyes. "I'd expect such infantile insults from such a bourgeois ignoramus."

"And I'd expect such a . . ." Tyler seemed to struggle for a good retort as Tammy Skiles walked past. A twinkle came to his eye. He pointed a finger in the air. And before Tammy could suspect a thing, Tyler was grabbing at the back of her shirt, finding the strap of her bra, and pulling it back like a slingshot.

*Snap!*

"Tyler!" She giggled.

Elijah simply shook his head in disgust. "Children," he muttered under his breath.

Washing his hands in the bathroom sink and watching bits of black paint escape down the drain, Elijah realized he was late for homeroom. Good, he thought. The more times he was late, the more the teachers would have to accept his tardiness. Before he knew it, he would be able to ditch classes and they wouldn't blink an eye.

It was a slow process, though, and he knew he had to ease into this rebellion. So he turned off the tap and hurried to Mr. Felton's room.

"Master Rosen," Mr. Felton bellowed as Elijah entered the room.

"Yes?"

"Is April twelfth your birthday?" Mr. Felton asked.

"You mean today?" Elijah said. "Not last time I checked."

"Oh," Mr. Felton deadpanned. "Because if it was, my present to you was going to be to excuse your tardiness. As it is, though . . ."

Felton took a black pen to his attendance book and, with an enthusiastic check, marked Elijah as tardy.

"So it goes," Elijah said, taking his seat.

He had read those words in a novel once, and he loved what they implied: Life was unfair. It came at you without a care. Things just happened and you couldn't do a darn thing about them. *So it goes*.

And so the day went. Elijah's first class was studio art, and as this was one of the few classes he still valued, he showed up on time.

Elijah was a writer at heart, a wielder of a pen. But he was also no slouch with a paintbrush. He often harbored dreams of painting covers to the books he would write. He already had a couple of titles picked out—*The Shadow of Dark* and *The Slow Death of Night*. The covers promised to require a lot of black paint.

His hope was to become a combination of all his favorite writers and artists, a creative superstar. He would sing in a gravelly voice like Tom Waits. He would challenge the system like Camus. He would attack canvasses like de Kooning. He had never actually seen a painting by de Kooning, but his art teacher, Mr. Lowe, had told him once that Elijah's own style was "vaguely reminiscent." So yes, he liked studio art.

After studio art came earth science. Earth science was a waste of his time. Earthquakes and volcanoes, ozone and oceans—who cared? Elijah figured that the way things were going in the world, we were going to blow it all up anyway. Why worry about how old the rocks are? The teacher, Mrs. Ruez, was nice enough, but Elijah sure wasn't going to start giving her the courtesy of showing up on time.

Ambling into class ten minutes late, he was greeted with Mrs. Ruez's disappointed frown.

"Elijah, Elijah, Elijah." She sighed. "We're all going to have to pitch in and get you a watch."

Elijah simply shrugged and dragged his feet toward an open seat in the back. Before he could sit, Mrs. Ruez spoke up.

"Not so fast, my friend. You'll be spending the morning at Mr. Snodgrass's office."

Elijah stopped and glared at her. "For being late?"

"Not this time," Mrs. Ruez said, a bit of sympathy leaking out of her voice. "He just called and wants to see you."

"Whatever," Elijah replied, turning around and dragging his feet back to the door. "Have fun learning about dirt, everyone."

In the hall, Elijah started to sweat. Rebels aren't supposed to sweat, he thought. But he couldn't help it. He was sure that someone had already discovered his initials spray-painted on the concrete behind the backstop. Snodgrass had been informed. The punishment would be swift and harsh.

Elijah had never really been punished. His rebellions were too small and adults were generally too supportive. Much to his disappointment, his parents loved his new look, his new attitude.

"It's good to show a little gusto," his father said to him once. "Did I ever tell you I went to see the Ramones? At a place in New York called CBGB. It was a—"

"I know what CBGB was," Elijah mumbled.

"Of course you do," his dad said with a smile. "You're a hip kid, aren't you?"

"Yes, Dad." Elijah sighed. "Very . . . hip."

When Elijah tried to rile teachers by wearing a Sex Pistols or a Buck Fush T-shirt, there was always more than one who gave him a thumbs-up. In a world of gold stars, it was hard work being controversial.

Graffiti was still controversial, though. And while it was exciting to tag a bit of concrete with his initials, he was starting to realize what rebellion really felt like. It felt like fear. Elijah wondered if Mahatma Gandhi had ever been scared when he was on a hunger strike, if Che Guevara had ever sweated when he gave a speech on social reform. When they'd been thirteen, they'd probably felt the way he did. They must have, he convinced himself.

Somehow, the halls of Ho-Ho-Kus Junior High felt different on the morning of April 12. Elijah couldn't place it, but the faux-marble floors and drab green lockers felt more sterile than usual. A big sign over the door to the cafeteria asked:

# READY FOR YOUR IDAHO TESTS?

Something about the font on the sign didn't sit right with Elijah. If he'd had to characterize it, he would probably have said it was a fascist font. He wasn't exactly sure what a fascist was, but he knew it had something to do with Nazis. It was a Nazi sign, then. A Nazi font.

This would be Elijah's fourth year of taking the Idaho

Tests. Each year, it became increasingly stressful. And as teachers constantly reminded the eighth graders, the previous years were little more than practice. The eighth-grade tests were the ones that mattered.

There was little doubt that Elijah would do well on the English section. He'd probably do all right on the rest of the sections too. His grades hadn't really slipped of late.

It was the actual taking of the tests that bothered him. They would all have to sit in the gymnasium, desk upon desk, and over the course of a day, they'd have to fill in bubble after bubble on Scantron sheets. Number-two pencils. A, B, C, or D? The purpose of the tests was to quantify everyone, to assign percentage points, to define kids with numbers.

It was enough to make him want to stand up and scream out something offensive—a howl of frustration or even a swearword. If he were allowed to skip them, he would. But they were mandatory, and as wonderful as it would have been to thumb his nose at the administration and sabotage the whole affair, he just didn't have it in him. After all, a silly sign made his heart race. How could he do something so revolutionary?

He pulled his eyes away from the sign and again took to the sterile halls. As he continued to wipe the sweat off his face, he told himself over and over, This is the price of greatness—the heavy, heavy price.

When he finally arrived at Snodgrass's office, he took a deep breath and held it, as if he were plunging into the cold ocean. He opened the door.

Three boys sat in chairs in front of Snodgrass's desk:

Denton Kensington, Wendell Scoop, and Eddie Green. It was an odd collection. Perhaps they were the informants.

Elijah slowly released his breath and looked at each of them with practiced disdain. As he sat down, he wondered if they were all sizing him up. Let them, he thought. Whatever they were there for, it didn't matter to him. I am, he told himself, a man who stands alone.

# Chapter 5

# BIJAY

As Bijay Bharata stepped off the school bus, he gazed longingly at the sign posted in front of Ho-Ho-Kus Junior High.

## Mackers arrives April 15th!

Just looking at it made him salivate. He loved Mackers. In his mind, Mackers was the best food in the world.

So what if his grandparents owned Taste of Delhi, the highest-rated Indian restaurant in northern New Jersey. Lamb vindaloo and chicken tikka masala were all well and good, but they had nothing on a Mackers Double Double

Triple. Two beef patties, two slices of cheese, three strips of bacon, and the perfect mix of pickles, onions, and secret sauce. He could drink that secret sauce, he adored it so much.

Bijay checked his watch to be sure. Only April 12—it was still three days away. The waiting was unbearable. True, there was a Mackers on nearly every corner in town, but having one at school was different. At home, Bijay was expected to eat traditional Indian fare, which he gobbled up with few complaints. But Mackers was strictly forbidden.

"That's not food," his grandmother would lament. "It's advertising."

Which was to say nothing of the fact that his grandparents were Hindu. While they let Bijay believe whatever he wished, they were never going to allow any beef in their home.

School was not home. All Bijay needed was five dollars in his pocket and he could have a daily fix. For pitching in at Taste of Delhi, he was given an allowance of twenty-five dollars a week. Things would work out. Three more days.

It was hard for Bijay to deny: he was round. Not just his belly, his entire body. He was shaped like a ball, unending curved edges. His face was round, and so were his hands and his feet. His nose was like a strawberry set below his eyes, which people always told him looked like the sparkling orbs of a cartoon character. This didn't bother him. He liked cartoons.

When he walked through the school's halls in the mornings, he smiled and said hello to nearly everyone. And nearly everyone said hello back.

But just two days ago, Sally Dibbs said something other than hello. She whispered, "They laugh at you, you know?"

She had a kind way about her, a tilting head and an airy voice. She dressed in flowing fabrics, as if she believed in fairy tales. But Bijay didn't understand why she insisted on commenting on every situation.

"Who laughs at me?" Bijay asked.

"Everyone," she said. "Because you're . . ."

"Husky?" Bijay said.

"Yes," she said, turning away. "And because you're . . . happy. They say hello because they feel sorry for you. Then they laugh because they can't believe you act like that."

"Maybe they're laughing at a joke they heard earlier," Bijay said. "Sometimes I'll watch a funny movie and laugh about it for days."

"Maybe they are, Bijay," she said with a curt nod. "You might be right . . . but I thought I'd tell you anyway. They laugh at me too, you know."

"Thanks, Sally," Bijay said. "Better not to worry about those things, right?"

As Bijay walked through the halls this morning, he *didn't* worry about what Sally had said. He smiled at people. He waved. He said hello. People returned the favor. And it felt good. Almost as good as food, movies, and theater, his other true loves. Greetings to Bijay were more than just formalities. They were an important part of a culture. They connected you to a place.

Bijay's soaring spirits dipped just a little when he

entered his first class of the day—math. He did fine in math, but it didn't interest him much. There was always a solution, a correct path. It didn't lend itself to imagination and improvisation. If he were to choose, every class of the day would be theater. But at Ho-Ho-Kus Junior High, theater classes were considered an extracurricular activity.

He had to wait until after school to indulge his dramatic ambitions. For the theater club, his latest role was that of the Cowardly Lion in *The Wizard of Oz*. Rather than simply copying the movie performance, Bijay was trying something different. He was giving the character an Indian twist, an accent and a Hindu mentality. The head of the theater club, Mr. Gainsbourg, had loved the idea and told Bijay to go for it.

Bijay drew on Bollywood for inspiration.

It was the movie industry of India, his parents' homeland, and while it might be meaningless to the rest of his peers, to Bijay it was a vital source of art. The movies of Bollywood were more plentiful and more joyous than those found in America. They were optimistic fantasies, where singing, dancing, and drama combined in a whirlwind of color. They were not unlike *The Wizard of Oz*.

So in the back of math class, Bijay hummed to himself and thought of how Bollywood legend Suraiya might sing "King of the Forest."

"Hey, Apu," came a voice from behind him.

Bijay turned around and received a pencil flick to the forehead from the one and only Tyler Kelly.

"Youch." Bijay rubbed his forehead and responded a bit too cheerily, "How's it going, Tyler?"

"Quit the hummin', Apu," Tyler said. "I'm trying to have myself a nice, peaceful nap."

"Okay, Tyler. I'm sorry."

Mrs. McAllister turned from the blackboard. "Tyler? Bijay? My guess is you're not discussing fractions."

"Ummm . . ." Tyler stalled.

"Tyler was . . . just helping me," Bijay said, saving the day. "This is difficult stuff, and he was just . . . explaining. He's quite good at math."

"Tyler is?" Mrs. McAllister asked with more than a hint of doubt in her voice.

"Of course," Bijay responded.

"Of course," Tyler seconded with a smile.

Shaking her head, Mrs. McAllister turned back to the board. "Let me handle the teaching, okay, fellas?" she said. "Eyes on the board."

As Mrs. McAllister chalked up the board with fractions, Tyler leaned over to whisper in Bijay's ear.

"Apu," he said faintly.

"Yes?"

"Don't expect me to thank you." And Tyler flicked him on the back of the head with his pencil, but lighter this time.

"You're welcome," Bijay whispered back.

Later that morning in English class, they were discussing *A Separate Peace*. It was a sad book, and everyone was analyzing the ending and describing how it made them feel. Some of the girls were getting tearful just thinking about it.

Bijay had read it, and appreciated it, but it didn't upset him at all. Maybe it was because he had lost things in life. When he was barely five years old, he had lost his parents.

*Lost,* that was the term teachers and counselors used, as if he'd misplaced them. He knew precisely where they were. Their ashes had been scattered in the Ganges River.

His grandparents, now his sole guardians, were a stern and traditional pair. Not unloving, but not outward in their affections. They would often remind Bijay to honor the memory of his parents. Bijay's main memory of his parents was of pleasant, soothing voices, but not much else. If he had lost anything, that was it—memories.

"Finny left Gene with many memories," Bijay offered as a counterpoint to all the doom and gloom in English class. "And to know at a young age what loss truly is, well, that's a great gift. It prepares you for life. In that way, it's a happy ending."

"Well put, Bijay," Mrs. Reed said with a respectful nod.

The class sat in silence, considering his comment. Then Bijay raised his hand. Mrs. Reed cocked her chin, acknowledging him.

"I find the ending of *How to Eat Fried Worms* much sadder," he added.

"You do?" Mrs. Reed responded.

"Oh yes, oh yes," Bijay went on, without sarcasm. "There are so many better ways to cook worms. So many better sauces you could use. It was a culinary nightmare."

The whole class erupted in laughter. Even Mrs. Reed chuckled a bit.

"I never thought of it that way," she said.

Bijay smiled and nodded with satisfaction. Then he raised his hand again.

"Go ahead, Bijay." Mrs. Reed smiled. "You're on a roll."

"Just the bathroom." Bijay smiled back.

With a bathroom pass in hand, Bijay wove his way through the halls of Ho-Ho-Kus Junior High. A sign confronted him as he entered the bathroom:

## Mackers makes lunch fun!

He shielded his eyes, trying to block temptation out of his mind. In the bathroom, he went about his business, humming to himself. On his way out, he put his hand back over his eyes and navigated through the sliver of images between his fingers. His grandmother had been partly right about Mackers—advertising was a big part of it. There was more to it than that, though. Even without the signs, it was hard to escape the memory of a Mackers meal. The memory was usually even better than the food itself.

His fingers still over his eyes, Bijay turned the corner in the hall and ran into something, or rather, someone.

"I'm sorry," he said, pulling his hand away.

Before him stood Vice Principal Snodgrass. A tall man with thinning hair and bulbous eyes, Snodgrass placed his hand upon Bijay's shoulder, revealing long, spidery fingers.

"Bijay Bharata," he said softly, almost apologetically. "Our resident thespian and film buff. Just the man I wanted to see."

"Oh . . ." Bijay started to blush. "Well . . . here—here I am."

"Yes, you are."

Bijay could feel Snodgrass's hand turning his shoulder and guiding him in the opposite direction of Mrs. Reed's classroom.

"I'm on my way back to English class." Bijay held his bathroom pass up as evidence.

"Not at the moment," Snodgrass said. "Let's just take a detour to my office. I've already made a call down to Mrs. Reed. Didn't want her to worry."

"Okay," Bijay said warily. "Have I won a prize or something?"

"A prize . . . that's very good." Snodgrass grinned, showing his large teeth. They were all perfectly straight, except for his right upper incisor, which was angled menacingly outward. "Just come along with me. I think you know what this is regarding."

Bijay had no idea what it was regarding, but he followed Snodgrass just the same. They snaked through the halls at a consistent but strangely plodding pace. If Snodgrass was trying to make Bijay more tense, it wasn't working. He smiled the whole way, admiring the various decorations in the hall, only averting his eyes when a hint of a Mackers poster came into view.

When they finally reached his office, Snodgrass opened the door and ushered Bijay in. Four heads swung around from four chairs. Denton Kensington. Wendell Scoop. Eddie Green. And Elijah Rosen. Plopping down in the one empty chair, Bijay gave them all a friendly wave.

"Hello, fellas!"

Fear ran through each boy's face as they looked past

him and up at a sneering Snodgrass, who was closing the door behind him and smoothly turning the lock.

"The Unusual Suspects," he said. "Together again."

Together again? What does he mean? Bijay thought. He hardly knew any of these guys.

Snodgrass circled around to his desk. He loomed over it for a few seconds, then he bent down behind it. He emerged a moment later holding a duffel bag, which he carefully unzipped and turned over.

A pile of cash came tumbling onto the desk. Five-, ten-, twenty-, even fifty-dollar bills. Hundreds, if not thousands, of dollars, more than Bijay had ever seen at one time. It was like a bed of lettuce, a heap of pickles.

"And you thought you'd get away with it, didn't you," Snodgrass said, looking them all over. "Well, you're not *that* smart."

# Chapter 6
# WENDELL

**A** pile of cash will buy a lot of video games, Wendell thought. Hours and hours of seclusion. If he'd been more aggressive, he might have grabbed it all and headed to the door with a "So long, suckers, I've got some Xbox to play!"

Instead, he stared at it and wondered what it could mean.

"A lot of money," Snodgrass said. "Two thousand nine hundred sixty-five dollars, to be exact. Split five ways, it comes to—"

"Five hundred ninety-three dollars each," Wendell said automatically.

"Exactly, Mr. Scoop, but you all would already know that, wouldn't you?" Snodgrass sneered.

"Is this the prize?" Bijay asked.

"What prize?" Denton jumped in.

Snodgrass laughed a little. "Don't play dumb with me, boys. The jig is up. You're caught. At least have the decency to admit what you've done."

"What have we done?" Eddie asked.

Snodgrass clucked his tongue disapprovingly and shook his head slowly. Then he opened his desk and removed a file folder. He smacked it down on the wood.

"Earlier this year, I had the police department come in and take fingerprints of everyone," he explained. "Do you remember that?"

"Of course we remember that fascist bull——" Elijah caught himself before he swore, but his anger couldn't be concealed.

"I did it," Snodgrass explained calmly, his reptilian eyes fixed on Elijah, "for your safety. Young kids go missing all the time. If you have their fingerprints, it sometimes can help an investigation. It can save lives. I never thought we'd be using them for this."

"And what exactly did you use them for?" Denton asked.

Snodgrass shook his head again, as if pitying him. He opened the folder and tossed stapled stacks of paper in front of each of the boys.

"You've all seen *CSI*?" he asked.

Wendell looked down at the papers. They were riddled with legal mumbo jumbo, black-and-white reproductions of fingerprints, and mathematical graphs that even he would have difficulty translating. He looked back up at Snodgrass.

"Well, it takes a little longer in real life," he went on. "But it's amazing what science can do. We've got the DNA evidence as well, if you want to see it. But fingerprints are so much easier to understand, especially for boys."

"Deoxyribonucleic acid," Eddie blurted out.

"Excuse me?" Snodgrass said loudly, shifting his gaze.

"DNA," Eddie whispered, "I understand what it is."

The vice principal's hand swooped down like a vulture toward Eddie's head. Eddie started to flinch but had nowhere to go. Snodgrass's talons found their way to a perch on Eddie's buzzed hair. He patted him lightly, as one might a small dog.

"Of course you do, Mr. Green," Snodgrass said softly. "And so you'll know that evidence of this sort is . . . incontrovertible."

"Incontri-what?" Bijay asked.

"Undeniable," Denton explained.

"I'm so glad I don't have to dumb it down for you fellas," Snodgrass said. "I'm too used to talking to Tyler Kelly."

This made Eddie chuckle a bit. Wendell knew a thing or two about Eddie—a troublemaker by reputation. He seemed harmless enough, but seeming was one thing and being was another.

"Something funny, Mr. Green?" Snodgrass asked.

"No, sir," Eddie said quickly.

"Good," Snodgrass said. "See, boys, Mr. Green has met with me before. The rest of you have not. Mr. Green knows I don't find mischief humorous. And crime, there is absolutely nothing funny about crime."

"I don't understand," Denton said. "What is this all about?"

"Look at the top of the papers," Snodgrass said stonily.

Wendell looked closer. In the top right-hand corner of the papers was his name, printed in a tiny font. These were his fingerprints. By the looks on the other boys' faces, he could tell they were looking at their own sets of fingerprints.

"Next time you plan on stealing money from the bake sale, boys," Snodgrass said, "wear gloves."

"Stealing?" Wendell said. The trouble he had wished for was now right in front of him, and it didn't feel liberating in the least. It felt like a hand around his throat.

"From the bake sale?" Bijay smiled, as if this were all a joke. "I would have taken brownies and Rice Krispies Treats, not mon—"

"This is preposterous," Denton said.

"How exactly is it preposterous, Mr. Kensington," Snodgrass said, "that after last week's bake sale, the entire profit of two thousand nine hundred and sixty-five dollars went missing?"

"Well, I had absolutely nothing to do with that," Denton said.

"Money." Elijah sniffed. "Who needs money?"

"So the bake sale was successful, then?" Bijay asked.

Snodgrass tossed a small piece of paper onto the desk.

"Two days after the sale," he said, "I received this anony-mous note."

# it WAs th℮ WOrK OF DwEEB

It was written with snippets of paper and glue, just like a ransom note. Only the letters weren't cut from magazines. They were quite clearly taken from school textbooks. Wendell tried to think of all the kids in school he'd seen defacing schoolbooks. Was Eddie one of them?

Eddie happened to be the first one to speak up. "So who's the dweeb?"

"You're the DWEEB," Snodgrass said. "All of you are."

"What in the heavens are you talking about?" Denton snapped as he jumped to his feet.

"Acronyms are nothing new to me," Snodgrass said, calmly motioning for Denton to sit. "Denton. Wendell. Eddie. Elijah. Bijay. Take the first letters of each of your names, put them together, and you have—"

"DWEEB!" Bijay announced happily.

"And when I found five hundred ninety-three dollars in each of your lockers, covered in your fingerprints . . . well, there's about one thing to assume," Snodgrass went on.

"Absurd," Denton grumbled, sitting back down.

"We don't even know each other," Elijah protested. "I've got nothing in common with these guys!"

"I'd expect you to deny it," Snodgrass said. "That's why I searched *everyone's* lockers. That's why I had the tests done. That's why I waited until all the evidence was in. It makes me sad to know that some of the school's best students could be involved in such an awful incident."

"That's right, we're top-notch students. Why would we ever be involved in something this dreadful?" Denton said.

"Even good students crack under pressure, or decide they're entitled to something they don't actually deserve," Snodgrass said. "I have to admit, the name of your little crime syndicate is clever. DWEEB. Very appropriate. Yes, you're clever boys. Criminal masterminds, though? Hardly."

"We were framed," Elijah spoke up. "This is a classic frame-up."

Wendell nodded in agreement. It reminded him of a video game he used to play, where the main character woke up in a hotel room with a bag of diamonds and no memory as to how he got there. The cops were on his trail, and his mission was to prove his innocence.

"Framed? A fine theory," Snodgrass said. "One I even entertained. But honestly, who would want to frame you?"

Wendell thought it over. Did he have any enemies?

Bijay proposed the only possible suspect. "Tyler Kelly?"

Snodgrass chuckled. "Tyler couldn't frame a picture."

He had a point. Fingerprints, DNA, piles of cash? Tyler wasn't capable of something so elaborate. And who had any reason to frame Wendell?

"I'd like to call my lawyer," Denton said.

"You're kidding, right?" Elijah scowled. "You have a lawyer?"

"This is no time for lawyers," Snodgrass said. "I haven't even contacted the police."

"Really?" Wendell asked.

"Of course," Snodgrass said. "I'd prefer not to make this public."

"Our parents?" Denton asked.

"They don't know a thing," Snodgrass explained. "And they don't have to. I have a proposition for you boys. Something to set things right."

Wendell turned to the others and they looked back warily. Snodgrass rose from his desk and straightened his wispy hair with his ghastly fingers.

"Come with me," he said.

Snodgrass led them out of the office, into the halls, then through a door marked STAFF ONLY; they marched carefully and silently in his wake. Behind the door was a massive room filled with boilers and pipes, the coughing lungs of the school. It was hot inside, but that didn't seem to bother Snodgrass at all. Wendell began to sweat.

In the back of the room was an orange door. Snodgrass pulled his hand into his sleeve, then raised it to a panel of numbers, shielding the panel from view. He punched in a code through the fabric, and a click followed. He hoisted the door open with his elbow, and cool but stale air poured out. He held his hands out, coaxing the boys through the door.

They walked single file down a set of stairs, Snodgrass at their heels. The stairs seemed to go on forever, down and down and down. Elijah might have been right about them barely knowing each other, but at that moment, Wendell was pretty sure the guys were thinking the same thing he was:

*Oh no, oh no, oh no, oh no . . .*

He wondered if one of the others might be tempted to make a dash for it. Only problem was, Snodgrass blocked their escape. They had no choice but to continue their descent.

When they finally reached the bottom, they gathered together on a small landing composed of a concrete floor. Skirting the bottom edge of the walls were small glowing lights, like the ones marking the aisles in movie theaters.

In the soft glow, Wendell could just make out Snodgrass's face. He couldn't read anything into it, not whether the situation gave him pleasure or filled him with fear. It was as if, in the darkness, Snodgrass stopped pretending to have emotions at all.

Again, he pulled his hand into his sleeve, cupped it over a panel of numbers, and typed in a code. There was another click. A hidden door without a handle popped out from the cinder-block wall, revealing a sliver of light. Snodgrass wedged his elbow into the crack and pried the door open. It sounded immensely heavy to Wendell, like the door to a bank vault, or maybe a tomb.

Snodgrass ushered them into a small room. A series of fluorescent lightbulbs lined the ceiling, flickering out a sickly light. Three bunk beds lined the wall. Five desks and five chairs were lined up in two rows, like a miniature classroom. The floor was concrete; the walls were cinder block. A tiny bathroom without a door extended out from the corner.

It was no bigger than Wendell's bedroom, and Wendell's bedroom was hardly big enough to contain him. Wendell took a deep breath of the stale air, hoping this was only a short visit.

He turned away from the others and focused his attention on a large poster that hung on the back wall. It was a photo of a man dangling off a cliff, hanging on by his fingertips. It read:

## PERSEVERANCE: What the mind can conceive and believe, it can achieve!

Snodgrass must have noticed, because he pointed up to the poster. "Believe it," he said.

Wendell stared at the image. Then he surveyed the room. With all the rumors and legends that made their way through the school, no one had ever mentioned a room like this. "What is this place?" he finally asked.

"Oh," Snodgrass said, "that all depends. It was built years ago. As a safe place. And it still is. But now I choose to look at it as your home."

"Pardon?" Denton said.

"Let's cut to the chase," Snodgrass said.

"Let's," Elijah echoed contemptuously.

Snodgrass ignored him and went on. "We all know what you did. And we all know it could land you in places you'd rather not be. The State of New Jersey has no problem sentencing children as adults. Especially for adult crimes—"

"But—" Denton tried to break in.

Snodgrass's calm tone shifted to something much louder and more manic. "But! Mr. Kensington! You will shut your limey mouth! And you will listen to me! Because I am here to save you boys! I am here to help you!"

Denton stepped back and slipped behind Wendell. It was almost as if he was expecting Wendell to protect him, but Wendell was just as tempted to step behind one of the other boys.

Snodgrass cleared his throat and continued in a softer but still frightening voice. "This is what's going to happen," he said. "I am going to call your parents and tell them you've all been accepted to Mensa. It's an organization for . . . well, let's just say the gifted. I'm sure you've heard of it. And I'm going to tell your parents that you've all been called away to a secret Mensa meeting in Montreal. That's in Canada. You know, the same place you tell everyone your girlfriends live!"

Snodgrass snapped his fingers to emphasize the joke. Wendell hung his head. It was hard enough dealing with the eighth grade without having your vice principal ridiculing your romantic prospects.

"I'm kidding, of course," Snodgrass continued. "Girlfriends are not your areas of expertise. But I know you're fine students. And because you're fine students, and because the Idaho Tests are coming next Friday, you're going to pay for your crimes in an appropriate way. For the next week you will live in this room. You will *stay* in this room. And you will do just one thing. You . . . will . . . study!"

"Is that right?" Elijah said, angling toward the door.

"And in a week," Snodgrass said, stepping in Elijah's path, "you will take the Idaho Tests. And you will, of course, get perfect scores. Do this for me . . . and all will be forgiven. And you will be released."

Wendell imagined what life would be like in the room. A week alone wouldn't be so bad. But with four others there, things would get . . . difficult. He wondered if they'd want to talk with him.

Wendell turned to Bijay, the one kind face in the room. Somehow, he had managed to keep smiling, even as he looked up at the completely manufactured poster.

"It's a nice poster," Bijay said to him.

"The poster," Snodgrass said, "will be your motto. And silence will be your promise. Now hand over the cell phones, gentlemen."

Snodgrass extended his hand. Denton was the first one to follow the command. As he dug into his pocket and handed off his iPhone, he said, "An entire week? Alone in here?"

"Oh, you'll be fed," Snodgrass explained as he collected the phones from the others. "Looked after. Trust me when I tell you this will be a lot more pleasant than a juvenile facility. Think of it as detention. A long detention."

"But we didn't do anything," Elijah insisted.

"Keep telling yourself that," Snodgrass said, moving over to the door. "Or feel free to tell the police. I'm sure they'll be sooo much more understanding than I am."

"Principal Phipps!" Eddie cried out. "We'd like to talk to him first! He'll straighten this out." Wendell nodded in agreement.

"That would be nice, wouldn't it." Snodgrass smiled. "Thing is, no one knows where he is. He disappeared. Took an unexplained leave of absence yesterday. Could be in Tahiti by now. That's right. . . ." Snodgrass spoke slowly, stressing each word as he said it. "Principal Phipps is gone."

"But . . . ," Eddie said, his voice deflating.

"But all you have for now is me," Snodgrass said. "And

all you have is this room. I'll be back in an hour, and I'd like a decision."

Before they could say another word, Snodgrass took a step backward through the door and violently pushed it shut.

Wendell stared at the door. He didn't move for close to a minute. When he finally turned to look at the others, he found them in the same position: frozen. Confused. Scared.

Then he heard something. Faint at first, but gradually getting louder. From deep within the walls . . .

*Grrrrrrrr* . . .

Wendell turned to Bijay quizzically. Then he slowly pointed to the boy's round belly. He crossed his fingers behind his back.

The well-worn smile fell from Bijay's face, and he sadly shook his head.

# Chapter 7
# DENTON

**D**enton sat on the edge of a bunk bed, dazed and quivering, wondering how his life had come to this. That morning he was a good student and, for the most part, a good citizen. Now he was a criminal. Accused criminal, anyway. Convicted one, really. Because what was this room if it wasn't a prison?

"This is a load of crap," Elijah said, jumping down from an upper bunk.

"Is that right?" Denton shot back. "How so? Because you expected to get away with it?"

"What?" Elijah said.

"Just admit it," Denton said dismissively. "You stole the money. You're the only one here who would do something so dreadful, what with your sloppy clothes and your . . . your frazzled hair."

"I think his hair looks cool," Bijay said.

"My frazzled hair?" Elijah said. "This is your evidence?"

"Well, what else am I to think?" Denton protested. "None of these other blokes would have done it!"

"Well, *this* bloke," Elijah said, pointing to himself, "is apparently a regular Al Capone. Because not only did I steal the money, I also framed all of you in the process. And why? So we could be locked in a tiny room together for an exciting week of Snodgrass's Vacation Study Camp. That about the gist of it?"

Denton shrugged. "Don't expect me to understand the whims of Americans."

"I knew a guy who once spent two weeks without ever leaving his attic," Bijay announced.

Denton paused. He wasn't sure he had heard Bijay right.

"But he might have actually been Cambodian . . . originally, anyways," Bijay explained. "He was trying to break the world record. Turns out the record for not leaving your attic is like fifty years, so . . . so . . . he wasn't very close."

Was this a joke? Denton had heard that Bijay was odd, the type of kid who whistled in class and said blissfully clueless things. Maybe it was all an act, like performance art. Or maybe he was slow. In either case, Denton had trouble trusting him. He had trouble trusting any of these guys.

"Well, I'd love to hang out down here for fifty years," Eddie said as he walked over to the door and gave it a firm push, "but what are our options?"

"Options?" Wendell said.

"Options. Bargaining points," Eddie said. "I really don't think any of us stole anything, but Snodgrass will be back soon. And you gotta deal with Snodgrass like it's all business."

"Well, I'm not about to get a mark on my permanent record," Denton said. He couldn't tolerate a mark on anything. Once, during lunch, he got a ketchup stain on his shirt. He retreated to the boys' bathroom, where he attempted to scrub it off in the sink. When it wouldn't disappear, he went straight to Nurse Bloom's office and told her he was sick to his stomach and needed to go home. He spent the rest of the afternoon studying in his bedroom, the embarrassing shirt relegated to the trash can.

"My grandparents *do not* approve of theft," Bijay said.

"So you guys are perfectly fine with this garbage?" Elijah asked. "Forgetting the fact that we're innocent?"

"Look at it this way," Denton said. "Any of you lads have a hot date in the next week? Me, I was planning to attend school, then go home and study for the Idaho Tests. I don't see how this is any different."

"We don't have a TV," Eddie pointed out.

"Or a computer," Wendell said.

"Or a fridge," Bijay said.

"Or any backbones!" Elijah shouted. "Come on, guys! Just 'cause he's vice principal doesn't mean he's got everything figured out. Something's not right and we have a chance to stand up."

"I've always thought you'd be better served by a Parliament, but America is still a democracy, is it not?" Denton said. "We should vote."

"That sounds fair," Wendell said.

"Of course it's fair." Denton bristled. "I vote that we stay down here, take the punishment, and emerge in a week—tougher, smarter, and free. No reason to risk our futures over this."

"And what if we all disagree with you?" Elijah said, turning to the others for support.

"Majority rules," Denton said. He held out his hands in what he hoped looked like a gesture of openness and generosity.

"I'd actually like to stay down here," Bijay stated.

"Really?" Elijah sighed.

"Honor is very important to my grandparents," he explained. "I want them to be proud of me."

"Trent never got in trouble," Wendell said.

"Who's Trent?" Elijah asked.

"My brother," Wendell said. "He also never got into Mensa."

"But we're not *in* Mensa," Elijah said. "We're in here."

"But they don't know that," Wendell said. "In here, we're geniuses. Up there . . . disappointments."

"Up there," Eddie said, "I could lose my spot on the team. I don't care about whether someone thinks I'm a genius or not. I just want to run. I'm staying."

Denton beamed. People were taking his side. His point of view was the most popular in the room.

Elijah bit his lip, took his glasses off, and rubbed his left eye. He paced over to the wall and began tapping it gently with the tip of his sneaker. "So it goes," he said softly, his head hanging limply.

"You're with us, then?" Denton pointed at him.

"If I stand alone . . . Man, I really should stand alone." Elijah turned around to face them, leaned his back against the wall, and slid down into a lump on the floor. "But we are pretty screwed, aren't we?"

Wendell nodded sympathetically.

"I was jumping the gun a bit with my accusations," Denton said, stepping forward and presenting his hand. He knew this was the right move. He had to show Elijah he could admit his mistakes and move on. That was the way to maintain control of the situation.

"That's for sure," Elijah said.

"How about this?" Denton proposed. "We accept Snodgrass's offer. We do what he asks. We study. But when we have a free moment, we put our heads together and figure out what happened. No harm in that."

Elijah looked up at Denton, then raised his hand and shook Denton's halfheartedly. When Denton tried to pull him to his feet, he withdrew his hand. "I'm staying on the floor," he said.

Denton nodded, stepped back, and took a seat at one of the desks. He was disciplined enough to suppress his satisfied smile.

"I bet it's all a big prank," Bijay said. "And Snodgrass

is going to step into the room with a fistful of balloons and a TV camera and we'll all have a big laugh."

Eddie patted Bijay on the back and said, "I know Snodgrass. Not *really* a balloon guy."

About an hour later, the door swung open and Snodgrass stepped into the room. A plastic bag, its handles stretching with the weight of something heavy, hung from the bend in his elbow. He lowered the bag to the floor, took a deep breath, and looked the boys over.

"So?" he asked.

When no one else moved, Denton stepped forward to be their spokesman. "So . . . sign us up for the full week . . . sir."

"The right choice," Snodgrass said.

"What's in the bag?" Eddie asked.

Snodgrass closed his eyes and sighed. "And you don't believe I was going to get to that, Mr. Green?"

"I'm sorry, but the general consensus is that I'm incorrigible," Eddie said.

"An understatement," Snodgrass responded. "What the bag contains, gentlemen, is your homework. So make yourselves at home. I'll contact your parents with the story we discussed. Coach McKenzie will be stopping by with your dinner. And I've asked Nurse Bloom to check in on you to make sure everyone is healthy. Rest assured, you've done the noble thing."

Elijah stared at the corner, not saying a word.

"Good day to you." With that, Snodgrass stepped out of the room and pushed the door shut.

Wendell crept carefully over to the bag and reached inside. His massive hands emerged holding a book. The title was written in large block letters:

**TWENTY YEARS OF IDAHO TESTS**

He tossed the book to Denton, but his aim was askew and it hit the wall and fell to the floor. Embarrassed, he picked it up and slowly handed it to him instead.

"Cheers," Denton said.

Then Wendell pulled more copies of the same book from the bag and handed them around. Pulling the last copy out and keeping it for himself, he took a seat.

"That's it?" Eddie asked.

Elijah looked down at his copy. "Yeah, like a thousand pages of test questions isn't nearly enough fun."

"Well," Denton said, setting his book on his desk and hoisting it open, "I don't know about you lads, but I'm getting started."

Of course he knew the whole situation was strange. Of course he knew it was wrong, but Denton focused his entire concentration on the book. Studying, he believed, would take his mind out of that room. It would connect him to something familiar and safe.

At first, the other boys examined the books cautiously from a distance, as if they were explosives. But before too long, they sat down, cracked the books open, and joined Denton. Denton was glad. Following the set path was important to him.

Some of the questions weren't particularly difficult for Denton:

**What are the three branches of American government?**
He knew the answer was *legislative, executive, and judicial*.

**What layer of the atmosphere lies above the troposphere?**
He knew the answer was *stratosphere*.

Others took a bit more effort:

**What is x in the equation $17x - 12 = 114 + 3x$?**
He was pretty sure the answer was *9*.

**Who wrote *The Count of Monte Cristo*?**
He really had no idea but guessed that the answer was *Alexandre Dumas*.

**What is the unit between two bars of music?**
He left this one blank.

Denton suspected the other guys might have a better grasp of these questions. If they pooled their knowledge, they probably could get the correct answer to every single one. Test taking was a solitary act, though. How else could you determine who was ahead, who was behind, who moved on and who didn't?

When the door burst open that evening, Denton looked up, his eyes blurry from staring at the book. A hulking figure clad in a baseball cap, a T-shirt, and gym shorts stared him down.

"First things first," announced Coach McKenzie. "You all disgust me! I'm saying that now and I'm hoping you remember it. Because if I had my way, you'd be on a one-way bus to the filthiest juvenile detention center in Jersey. Common thieves! In my school! And you, Peter Pan? I figured you a bit fancy, but a thief? I'm appalled."

"But—" Denton began.

"Zip it," McKenzie said firmly, and he pointed to each boy individually as he kept talking. "Shut it. Button it. Velcro it. Whatever the heck kids do to it these days to *keep . . . it . . . quiet*! I'm talking, you're listening, and I'm only saying things once. Snodgrass wants you locked down here and I do not question orders. And neither will you."

Coach McKenzie pulled a paper bag out from behind his back and set it on the floor.

"Menu tonight: beef, broccoli, rice, milk. Mind and body, brain food, dinner of champions. You will eat it. You will say yum-yum. And when I return tomorrow morning, it will all be gone and you will rub your bellies and exclaim 'Gosh, Coach McKenzie, that dinner sure was swell!' Copy?"

Denton nodded nervously. He had come to fear McKenzie's military bluster. When he first started at school, he thought it might all be an act, a parody of a macho American man. It came so naturally, though, so forcefully, that he decided it was the man's essence. And he had no idea what it took to become someone like that.

"For the next week, I will not be teaching gym classes," McKenzie continued. "Coach Walsh will do double duty. My mission? I will be stationed on the other side of that door. I will be listening. And I will be checking in. You need me? You knock five times. I'll be in here faster than quick. But at night, I *will* be asleep."

From the pocket of his striped athelitc shorts, Coach McKenzie pulled a small electronic device and held it up for all to see.

"In the case of an emergency, you press the red button. I'll be bunking in my office. An alarm will go off and I'll be down here with a head full of steam and a genuine hope that an ambulance is gonna be called. Because the only type of emergency I believe in is the one that requires an ambulance. I don't read bedtime stories and I don't do room service. This button is only pressed when someone's frothing at the mouth."

He tossed the device to Eddie, who caught it but didn't look at it. He kept his eyes on McKenzie.

"Last things last. There are cameras all over this school. They're always watching. Day and night and night and day. If you Harry Potter your way into the hall, we're gonna know. It's a week, fellas, hardly any time at all. Crack those books but don't crack wise, and you'll get through this just fine."

Cocking his chin, McKenzie pivoted on one heel and headed back toward the door.

"Lights-out at nine-thirty. There will be no discussion on that matter. And I do not want anyone telling me he's innocent. You know who says they're innocent? Guilty people."

Denton's emotions told him to speak up, to argue, to once again proclaim his innocence, but he stayed silent. Denton knew that McKenzie had once been a marine. McKenzie's point of view, and everything else about him, was unwavering. Some teachers listened to reason and

Denton was adept at convincing them of his point of view. But to go head to head with McKenzie in an argument would be like trying to convince a lion he needed a haircut—a dangerous and useless course of action.

"Good night, boys," McKenzie said, stepping back through the door. "Sleep softly . . . and study hard."

As soon as McKenzie was gone, Bijay was upon the food. He was careful to hand it out evenly to everyone, but Denton could see that his body was shaking with hunger. Denton wasn't hungry, but he hadn't eaten all day, so he took his portion to a desk and picked at it.

He watched the others eat. Bijay tried to hold himself back at first, but before long he was piling the food into his mouth like a dump truck. Wendell chomped away sloppily, licking and smacking his lips. Elijah winced with every bite as if it were full of poison. Eddie spent most of his time moving the food around his paper plate with his plastic fork.

Denton was an only child. He had never been to camp, never shared a room with anyone. He hadn't even been to a sleepover before. So he wasn't sure what to expect after dinner. Were they supposed to sit around chatting? Who would decide on when to go to bed?

As soon as they finished their food, he got his answer. Elijah climbed into a bunk and pulled a pile of covers up over himself.

"I guess it's bedtime," Wendell said, following Elijah.

"Will there be more growling?" Bijay asked.

"I don't know," Eddie said. "I haven't heard anything. I don't want to hear anything."

"It was imaginary, I'm sure," Denton said uneasily.

"I guess we all share an imagination," Elijah called out from his bunk. "If you're going to say such stupid things, then just shut off the lights. I'll sleep all week if I have to."

As the others crawled into their bunks, Denton stood still. He wasn't tired. His mind was bursting. He knew Elijah was right—the growling wasn't imaginary. This punishment was completely unreasonable.

But he tried to dispel such thoughts from his mind. If he was going to follow his own advice and spend an entire week down here, he couldn't be distracted.

Denton switched off the light and fumbled into his bunk. He lay there in the dark, his eyes wide open.

He stayed that way for nearly an hour, until the growl behind the wall returned, rumbling up through the silence. On its heels came the sound of gentle weeping.

Denton shut his eyes and put his hands over his ears.

# Chapter 8
# EDDIE

**S**aturday morning couldn't come too soon. Eddie had hardly slept a wink. There were moments when he had dozed off for a few minutes, but then he'd jolt back awake as soon as he remembered where he was.

At 6:00 a.m. he got down from his bunk, went to the bathroom, then took a seat at one of the desks. He didn't turn on the lights for fear it was against McKenzie's rules. The others followed soon after. They didn't touch the lights either; they just sat there in the dark. Their yawns and grumbles told Eddie that it had been a rough night for everyone.

At 7:00 a.m. the door opened, the lights flickered on,

and there was McKenzie. The stripes on his shorts were red today instead of yesterday's blue. His T-shirt was his standard-issue coal gray.

"Morning, gents," Coach McKenzie said. He picked up the empty bag from the night before and placed a fresh one on the floor. "I trust you slept well."

Eddie nodded wearily. He had learned to function on just a few hours of sleep. Five hours kept his mind humming, his memory razor sharp. But if he got no sleep, the neurons didn't fire right.

The witty retorts weren't coming. Nodding was the best he could do. McKenzie clucked his tongue and shot an index finger at Eddie. In Eddie's dazed state, he couldn't tell whether this gesture was a taunt or a vote of support.

"Rock and roll," McKenzie said. "For breakfast we got hard-boiled eggs. We got bananas. We got yogurt. We got OJ."

"Oh! I almost forgot," Bijay said suddenly, then cleared his throat. "Gosh, Coach McKenzie, that dinner sure was swell!"

McKenzie froze and squinted. He leaned in, placed his hands on Bijay's desk, and got a close look at him. Eddie held tight to the side of his desk, not sure what might come next. What came next was a smile, like a slice of watermelon across McKenzie's face.

"A man who follows orders," he said firmly, "is a man who will go far. A man who can eventually give orders. Well done, Bharata! You ain't all songs and cupcakes, are you?"

"No, sir," Bijay said with a small smile.

"Excellent, excellent." McKenzie then returned to the door and pulled a piece of luggage into the room. He tossed it onto a bunk. Then he grabbed another bag, and another, and another, and finally one more, until five bags were resting on five bunks.

"Your parents packed up a week's worth of clothes for you. Toothbrushes, toothpaste, so on and so forth. Why they agreed to this punishment, I haven't a clue."

"Just a moment," Denton said. "Snodgrass didn't tell you the Mensa story? Canada? I mean, he was supposed—"

"He was supposed to tell me what I need to know and that's it," McKenzie snapped back. "I know you boys are guilty. Heck, I was with Snodgrass when he searched the lockers. That's all that's important. And I'm not listening to anything else."

McKenzie stomped to the edge of the room, and just before he left, he said, "I'll be back with your lunch. But now, you study."

And study they did—Denton made sure of it. Even when Wendell tried to take a break and go through his luggage, Denton scolded, "Time for that later," then pointed to the books. Eddie found his attitude a little condescending, but Denton was right. An entire week indoors seemed like an eternity. The only way to fill the hours was by studying.

Eddie's eyes looked down at pages. His hands turned them. Algebra and the Revolutionary War, vocabulary and biology and health and just about everything else an eighth grader was "supposed" to know. He tried his best to concentrate.

Just before lunchtime, McKenzie returned, and held a makeshift gym class by leading them in calisthenics—jumping jacks, squat thrusts, and an excruciating set of sit-ups. The others groaned through it all, but to Eddie it was a welcome change.

Then McKenzie served a lunch of turkey sandwiches and juice. At one o'clock he put them back to work. This, Eddie assumed, was what the rest of their sentence would be like. Days and nights completely dictated by routine. It was a strange sort of awful. Eddie, like anyone, relied on routines—in his training, in his diet. But there was always the opportunity to improvise.

Improvisation in this room was impossible. It was just cinder blocks, and desks, and bunks, and books. Eddie had two options: he could either study or stare at the poster on the wall. That stupid poster. Perseverance? Being bored wasn't perseverance. Perseverance was running a race with your ankles covered in blisters. Perseverance was the opposite of doing exactly what was expected of you.

It was late in the afternoon when the rush of air from the door opening roused Eddie from his book, and Nurse Bloom quietly stepped inside. Eddie was glad to see a face belonging to someone other than McKenzie or Snodgrass, but that face was all terror—brow up, lips fallen, eyes wide. Without making a sound, Bloom mouthed, "What in the . . . ?"

Slinging her purse over her shoulder, she made a bee-line for the back of the room, whispering "Back here" as she passed in between their desks. She crouched down and opened her arms, calling everyone into a huddle. They all rose from their desks and joined her.

"Is it true?" she whispered.

"That we did it?" Denton said. "Of course not."

"What if we *did* do it?" Wendell posed, his face flushed with excitement.

"But we *didn't* do it," Denton said, annoyed.

"For how long are you down here?" Bloom asked.

"For like a week," Eddie responded sadly.

"A week," Nurse Bloom whispered sympathetically. "Oh, you poor guys."

"Uh-huh," Elijah said dryly. "Supposedly this is better than sticking up for ourselves."

"Yeah, fellas," Nurse Bloom said. "If you didn't do it, why not just say it?"

"It's not that simple," Denton explained. "Snodgrass has ridiculous piles of evidence. We certainly don't look innocent."

"And if we do this," Bijay said, "everything will be fine. It's not so bad down here, you know."

"Oh no, it's horrible," Bloom said. "I'm going to talk to Snodgrass. Surely this is all a mistake. We'll have you home to your parents this evening."

"Really?" Elijah said, a rare smile breaking over his face. "That would be amazing."

"Count on it," Bloom said.

"But you should know that we're willing to stay,"

Denton chimed in, "should the situation prove a tad dicey. We have reputations to uphold."

"Well, let's worry about things getting dicey when they get dicey," Nurse Bloom said. "And let's worry about you guys right now. So how's everybody feeling?"

Eddie shrugged limply. Physically, he felt tired. Emotionally, he felt tired. Did she have a cure for tired?

With a firm "hmmm," Bloom stood up and walked over to one of the bunks and sat down on the mattress. At her side she set her purse, a hefty piece of expensive-looking white leather.

Eddie stared at the bag as Nurse Bloom reached inside. She pulled out a stethoscope and placed it on the bunk. Then she pulled out a sphygmomanometer.

Most kids probably didn't know what a sphygmomanometer was. Eddie knew well—every time he went to a doctor, they wrapped one of these things around Eddie's arm, pumped it up, and measured his blood pressure. He hated it.

"All right," Bloom said. "Who's first?"

"For?" Elijah said.

"I just want to check that you're all in good health," she said. "I wouldn't be fit to wear this if I didn't." She tugged at the lapel of her white lab coat.

Wendell coughed back his excitement and started to step forward.

Through his exhaustion, Eddie felt a surge of nervous energy. He slipped past Wendell and sat down next to the nurse.

"Fire up that sphygmomanometer, lady," he said, holding his arm out.

"Impressive," she said. "You know what it's called."

"Only an idiot wouldn't," Eddie said nonchalantly. "I'll spell it for you if you want."

She laughed. "That's okay. I wouldn't know if you're right or wrong. I'm a terrible speller."

Then she pressed the stethoscope to Eddie's chest, wrapped the sphygmomanometer around his arm, and began pumping it up.

He watched it with disdain. It wasn't bravery that made him go first. It was closer to the opposite. Doctors, nurses, medicine, they were speed bumps in life. Best to just get past them and move on.

Deflating the sphygmomanometer with one hand, Bloom reached into her purse with the other and pulled out a disinfectant wipe and a syringe.

"Whoa!" Eddie said, pulling his arm back. "I didn't sign up for that!"

"I know, I know, I'm an evil witch," Nurse Bloom teased. "There's nothing I enjoy more than making sure that little boys have functioning livers and kidneys."

"Liver and kidney function *is* quite important," Denton remarked. "I have mine tested frequently."

"Fine," Eddie said, giving her his arm back and closing his eyes. "If Oliver Twist can take it, so can I. But as they say at track meets: make it quick."

"Don't worry," she said. "This is one of the few things I do well. I've never been a genius, like you guys. But what I do, I try to do my best. I have to say, I do admire each one of you for being exceptional in your very own way. Together you'd be unstoppable."

Bloom cleaned the crook of Eddie's elbow with the wipe, and in one fluid motion, expertly inserted the needle. As she drew back the plunger, the syringe filled with blood so vibrant and red it seemed to bring an extra glow to the drab room.

# Chapter 9
## BIJAY

Nurse Bloom made a promise before she left. "This evening, tomorrow morning at the latest, we'll get you out of here."

It was a comforting thing for Bijay to hear. He had been to Nurse Bloom's office only once, after he nearly fainted in social studies. But from that one visit, he had come to know Nurse Bloom as a comforting person.

"Who sends their son to school with a fever?" she had said, her cool wrist against Bijay's radiating forehead.

"Grandson," Bijay clarified.

"Oh, that's right, sweetie," Nurse Bloom said. "You live with your grandparents, don't you?"

Bijay nodded. "They didn't send me with a fever. I just didn't tell them."

"Oh, Bijay," Bloom said. "You really should. It's important."

"I'm not supposed to whine about things," Bijay said. "I'm one of the lucky ones, you know?"

"You're lucky this is just a tiny fever," she said with a concerned frown. "But I'm still going to call your grandparents. You'll need to spend the rest of the day in bed. And if this fever gets any worse, you're going to have to call a doctor."

"Yes, ma'am," Bijay said.

"Bijay," she said, looking him in the eyes, "just because you're young doesn't mean you aren't important. It doesn't mean you don't deserve only the best. Remember that for me."


Sitting and eating dinner with the other boys now, Bijay had nothing but faith in Nurse Bloom. She seemed the type to keep her word.

"This would be the part in the Bollywood movie for the big song." Bijay smiled.

"The big song?" Denton asked.

"The finale," Bijay explained. "Dancing, streamers, fireworks, the whole shebang."

"I'm not singing until I'm aboveground and on my own again," Elijah said, poking at his food.

"You heard what Nurse Bloom said, right?" Bijay asked.

"That's right," Wendell seconded. "She'll be back for us."

But Nurse Bloom didn't return that evening. They waited patiently. They didn't even open their luggage.

By nine-thirty, the lack of sleep from the night before had taken its toll. Bijay couldn't concentrate. He could hardly talk to the others. He climbed onto a bunk and fell asleep on top of the covers.

Bijay had never cared for his dreams. They were anxiety-filled fables, the type of heart-thumping nightmares about coming to school naked, missing tests, suffering through horrible embarrassments. He woke up every morning and thanked his lucky stars that he didn't live in the world of his dreams.

The dreams he had Saturday night were no different. If anything, they were even more awkward and intense.

When he woke on Sunday morning and looked around the room at the cinder blocks and the desks, he was still thankful, but just barely. The dreams didn't seem so horrible when compared to reality. Bloom hadn't come, and to Bijay that meant only one thing: something terrible had happened to her.

"Maybe Snodgrass fired her," Eddie posited as they sat at their desks thumbing through their books.

"Maybe worse," Elijah said.

McKenzie came and went. The studying continued. And as the day wore on, Bijay grew more nervous. He kept worrying about Bloom. He felt as if his body would burst.

It was affecting the others too. Denton was the first to crack. "You stink!" he hollered at Wendell, slamming his book closed.

"Me?" Wendell said, cowering in his chair.

"I'm sorry, Wendell," Denton said, "but you're like a frankfurter dredged in Marmite. Simply rancid."

Bijay couldn't look at them. He didn't know why Denton insisted on criticizing everyone. And he hated that Wendell never stood up for himself.

"My . . . BO?" Wendell asked softly.

"I know we don't have a shower," Denton said, "but you could at least change your clothes."

"I could . . . do . . . that," Wendell said.

Bijay looked up to see Wendell quietly pace across the room, pull his bag down from his bunk, and open it up. He seemed to be keeping his composure, but when he opened his bag, his face changed. His eyes became watery.

He lifted a piece of paper from the bag, unfolded it, and read quietly to himself.

"What is it?" Bijay asked.

"Just a note . . . from my parents," Wendell said, coughing back his emotion. He folded the paper up and stuffed it in his pocket.

"Would you read it to us?" Bijay asked.

"I'd rather not."

The other boys sprung from their seats immediately and attacked their bags, jiggling the zippers and struggling with the buckles to get them open as fast as possible.

They retrieved their own letters, and hurried back to their desks to read them in privacy. Bijay watched as they smiled to themselves and took their time reading them over and over again. He stood up and went to his bag. He carefully sifted through his clothes, knowing what he would find.

After a few minutes, Eddie walked up to Bijay, who was still standing at the bunks empty-handed.

"What does your letter say?" Eddie asked.

"My grandparents don't really write letters," Bijay said with a shrug.

"Do your parents write them?" Denton asked.

"My parents are dead," Bijay said plainly, and he immediately regretted it.

"Oh," Denton said as he tried to hide his own letter behind his back. "I'm—I'm dreadfully sorry to hear that. Forgive me, Bijay, I didn't know."

"That's cool. I hardly knew them. So it isn't really sad," Bijay said. His intention was not to make Denton feel awkward; he was just relaying information.

"In Bangladesh people still die of diseases that are preventable. Is that true for India as well?" Denton asked carefully.

Bijay nodded. "They do. They die of things like cancer too. Like anywhere."

"Oh," Denton said, his face turning pink.

"Yeah . . ." Bijay trailed off.

Bijay loved to perform onstage, but when it came to his real life, he felt guilty being the center of attention. He thought of walking back into the bathroom to be alone, but it wasn't even private back there. The only place for privacy was outside of the room. With no Nurse Bloom to help them, it would be days before he would see the other side of the door. Reality had truly sunk in.

McKenzie brought their dinner in the early evening. It was uninspired, a mix of roasted chicken, steamed spinach, and boiled potatoes.

The chicken was dry and the potatoes were flavorless.

The spinach was spinach. Bijay took a feeble bite, then dropped a drumstick onto his plate and looked over at the books. There were still hundreds of pages to get through.

If his grandparents knew what he was doing, they would be ashamed. How on earth would anyone be proud of him for going along with this? It was enough to make him want to gorge himself on fifty Double Double Triples.

"You know, if we were in school tomorrow, we would be eating Mackers," Bijay said. "But all we have is this junk."

"My mom makes tacos on Sundays," Wendell said. "I love taco night."

Denton stopped eating. He dropped his knife and fork onto his plate and stood up. "They knew!" he yelled.

"Shh," Eddie whispered. "You'll put McKenzie on the warpath."

"How did I not think of this earlier?" Denton said, still worked up but trying to keep his voice down.

"Think of what?" Elijah said.

"My parents," Denton went on. "They knew we were in trouble even before we did."

Bijay wasn't sure what Denton was getting at, but he saw Eddie's face light up in recognition.

"I hate to say it, but he might be right," Eddie remarked. "Mine did too. My dad gave me fifty bucks before I left. He doesn't normally do that. Why would he do that?"

"And my mum kept on about how Friday was supposed

to be the most delightful day in my life," Denton exclaimed. "What was she on about? Good lord, I think I'm going to vomit."

Bijay couldn't exactly relate. When he left for school on Friday, he hadn't spoken to his grandparents. He hadn't spoken to anyone.

"You're saying they set us up?" Elijah said. "I don't know. My parents annoy me, but I don't think they'd do that."

"I don't know what they've done," Denton said. "I'm just saying they knew something. In their letter to me, they wrote that I 'deserve' this. Deserve a reward or deserve a punishment? Who knows?"

Wendell stood up and walked over to the wall. He stared at the Perseverance poster.

## PERSEVERANCE: What the mind can conceive and believe, it can achieve!

The picture of the man dangling over the cliff didn't mean much to Bijay. But to Wendell, it seemed to inspire pure anger. His hands were clenched into fists, and as he squeezed them tighter, the blood drained away, making them pale and blotchy.

"Wendell?" Bijay said.

Wendell's stare didn't budge, but he started speaking softly. "These zits on my face," he said, "I woke up with them on Friday. I didn't want to come to school, but Mom insisted. 'Those zits won't mean much where you're going,' she said. *Where you're going.*"

"Wendell," Elijah said. "Let's think about this. We don't know what they were talking about. We don't know anything."

Wendell turned his head. "They were saying goodbye."

"That's not—" Bijay started to say, but the sound of Wendell's fist pounding the poster cut him off.

"This! Is! Such! Crap!" Wendell yelled. With each word, he pounded the poster with his clenched hand. The last punch sank in deeper than the rest and the sound of scraping concrete followed.

No one moved. Wendell pulled his hand back and began rubbing it. A look of guilt settled on his face. Then he reached forward cautiously, pulled the bottom of the poster up, and peeled it from the wall.

Behind the poster, Bijay could see a loose cinder block, sunken in deeper than the rest. Wendell pushed it gently. It slid back until it fell into the space behind the wall, landing on the ground with a crash.

"I'm sorry. I'm so sorry," Wendell said, hurrying to the door. He braced himself against it. "We're in trouble, aren't we? We're in big trouble."

"We're fine," Bijay said hesitantly. He started to reach his hand out to Wendell, then pulled it back. He wasn't sure what to do.

Wendell waited for a few seconds, then flipped the light switch off.

In the dark, Bijay could hear Wendell shuffle past. The bunk creaked as he climbed up into it. Then there was silence once again.

"Um," Eddie said, "what are you doin', Wen?"

All Wendell would say was "I'm so sorry . . . I'm so sorry" in a low, trembling whisper.

After a while, Bijay whispered back, "It's okay, everything will be fine." He doubted anyone heard him, though. He was really just saying it to himself.

# Chapter 10
## ELIJAH

"**W**e should go," Elijah said. He rolled over, wrapping the covers around himself until they formed a tight cocoon. He faced the wall, but it was too dark to see anything.

"We should sleep," Denton said.

"Now's our chance," Eddie said, from the bunk below Elijah. His voice was fully charged. He seemed genuinely excited by the danger of the situation.

"Our chance for what?" Denton said. "Once we get out, what do we do?"

"We don't know what's back there," Wendell said.

"We—we—we—" Bijay stuttered.

"We should sleep," Denton said definitively.

The whispers bounced back and forth in the darkness until they faded off to silence. It didn't matter anyway. Elijah was tired of debating. He just wanted to get out and let fate decide what happened next.

When the others fell asleep, he'd just take the poster down, and stick his head behind the wall and see what they were dealing with. He hadn't forgotten about the growling, though. So better yet, he'd wake up Eddie and ask him to do it. Eddie was willing to do anything.

It was a fine plan. Except for the fact that Elijah fell asleep about ten seconds after formulating it.

He woke on Monday morning to the sound of Denton screaming "Bloody 'ell!"

The Perseverance poster lay splayed out on the floor. A pair of running shoes were poking out from the hole in the wall. Denton was grasping at the laces.

"Lay off!" came Eddie's voice.

"What are you thinking?" Denton said.

"I'm thinking I'm gonna see what's back here." The shoes slipped free from Denton's hands, and the sound of Eddie's body collapsing into the space behind the wall roused Wendell and Bijay from their bunks.

"Sonuva . . . ," Eddie grumbled.

"So . . . what's—what's back there, then?" Denton asked as Elijah slipped on his glasses and joined his side.

"Pipes," Eddie responded. "Yeah, mostly pipes. I think I can climb 'em, though." Wendell and Bijay got up and joined the others next to the hole.

"You can get out, then?" Elijah asked. He placed an ear

against the wall and closed his eyes, trying to imagine what Eddie might be seeing.

Before Eddie could respond, the sound of the lock on the door clicking open stopped them in their tracks. Elijah found himself acting with surprising speed, grabbing the poster and pushing it against the wall to cover the hole.

"Men!" McKenzie bellowed, stepping inside. "Morning has broken. Breakfast is served." Placing the breakfast on the floor, he turned toward them.

"Morning," Denton said with a guilty smile.

McKenzie eyed the cockeyed poster with interest. He finally said, "Not a bad little slogan. But not as good as Semper Fi. Know that one?"

"It's from your hat," Bijay said, pointing to McKenzie's black cap, which was emblazoned with the words in yellow thread.

"It's from Latin," Elijah informed Bijay. "*Semper Fidelis*. Means 'always faithful.' "

"It's from the marines," McKenzie clarified. "Means stay true to your brothers. Don't leave the corps. And don't you ever leave any man behind. Speaking of which . . ."

McKenzie stepped over to the bunks and looked them up and down. "Where in God's name is Green?"

Dead silence. For what seemed like . . . forever.

Eyebrow cocked, McKenzie continued, "Green? Your good buddy Eddie?"

Elijah shrugged feebly, but his insides were pulsing and throbbing and he felt as if he were about to scream. Once McKenzie discovered they had broken the rules, what punishment could possibly come next?

"*Where . . . is . . .*" McKenzie's voice cracked as he started to shout.

"Having a bit of an issue, Coach."

McKenzie turned toward the bathroom. It lacked a door, but the toilet was hidden behind the wall in an alcove.

"You're okay?" McKenzie called.

Elijah held his breath.

"Yeah," came Eddie's voice again, "just a little stomach thing. I'd steer clear of here for a bit. But I'll be fine."

"Good to hear, good to hear. I'll give you guys some credit. You're toughing it out. I'll be back to check on you later, then."

"I'd appreciate that, thank you," Eddie called back.

McKenzie gave the rest of them a respectful nod. Still stunned, Elijah nodded back.

"Carry on, soldiers," McKenzie said. "Carry on." And he smiled. It wasn't McKenzie's typical smile, either. If Elijah were to describe it, he'd say it was almost kind.

After McKenzie left, they all scrambled to the bathroom, only to find it empty.

"Eddie?" Denton said.

"Yup," Eddie's voice came from the toilet.

"Where are you?" Elijah asked, crouching down and looking behind the porcelain tank.

"Just hanging with the toilet pipes. You can crawl all over the place back here."

"That was far too close," Denton said. "Now get back in the room."

"I thought I might explore a bit. It's real dark, but I might be able to find my way out."

"You should probably come back," Wendell said.

"I will, I will, it's just—"

*Grrrrrrrrrr!*

Because of the hole in the wall, the growl was twice as loud as it had been before. Because Eddie was back there, it was also ten times more frightening.

"Eddie!" Elijah yelped. Encouraging their escape suddenly seemed like the stupidest thing he could have done. Now Eddie could suffer from Elijah's selfish decision.

"Okay, I'm coming, I'm coming!" Eddie said frantically.

Clinking and bumping and scraping sounds telegraphed Eddie's path as he scrambled along the walls back to the hole. Bijay pulled the poster down.

*Grrrrrrrrrr!*

To Elijah, it sounded as though the growl was getting closer, but he wasn't going to wait around and see. As soon as Eddie's hands sprouted from the hole, Elijah grabbed them.

"Pull, pull!" Eddie called.

Getting Eddie through the hole was like removing a nail from a board. It required so much twisting and yanking that Elijah wondered how he had gotten in there in the first place.

"Pull!" Eddie begged, the growling remaining loud and constant.

Finally, Eddie sucked in his breath and his torso slid slowly along. Once Eddie's hips were free, Elijah gave a hefty tug and brought him toppling into the room.

"Thank you, thank you," he said breathlessly.

Bijay replaced the poster, and Elijah stared at it, almost expecting it to fly off the wall and reveal some terrible monster. Hands up, he backed away and sat on the bunk. The others joined him.

After a few minutes, the growling faded until it was gone. They waited for nearly an hour and it didn't return. Things seemed safe, at least for now, but the whole incident scared Elijah more than he cared to admit.

He held tight to the edge of his bunk, trying to keep his hands from shaking. And in his head, he couldn't get rid of the memory of a voice: Tyler Kelly's voice. It kept saying the same thing, over and over again.

"Maybe I should call you Eliza?"

Though he wasn't quick to admit it these days, Tyler Kelly had once been Elijah's friend. One of his best friends, actually. They had known each other since first grade.

Throughout elementary school, they weren't much more than a couple of guys who had lunch together. But by sixth grade, they were inseparable, and spent almost every afternoon hanging out in Tyler's basement wolfing down junk food. They would make up wild stories, making fun of everyone they knew and imagining a world where they were the school's dictators of style and substance.

Tyler wasn't quite as creative as Elijah, but his humor was nastier, and just listening to him skewer their peers made Elijah feel as if he were doing something wrong. But it also felt good. It was a safe version of wrong.

In seventh grade, things got a bit more dangerous. When Tyler found out how to program his cell phone to display as a restricted number on caller ID, he brought back an ancient art—the prank call.

No one was off-limits. Classmates. Parents. Teachers. Tyler would call them all and, adopting a false voice, he'd say all the things the two of them used to say in the privacy of the basement.

At first, it was exciting for Elijah, because Tyler was the one doing the dirty work. The more he did it, though, the more uncomfortable it made Elijah feel. And the more confidence it seemed to give Tyler.

Then one day during lunch, Tyler sat down next to Elijah and made an announcement. "Sara Childs and Emma Radson are swinging by my basement after school. They want you to be there."

"But we hate them," Elijah said. It was true that Sara Childs and Emma Radson, two of the school's most popular girls, were often the victims of Tyler's prank calls.

"We don't hate them if they're coming over," Tyler explained, wagging his fist like a champ. "Come on, man, do you realize what this means?"

"What does it mean?" Elijah asked.

"These girls think we're a couple of guys who know a thing or two about a thing or two!" Tyler exclaimed. "And now they want to show their appreciation."

"Their appreciation?"

"You know what I mean," Tyler said. "Come on, hot shot. They want to see me do one of the calls. Principal Phipps. The big fish."

"I don't know," Elijah said. "Not really my scene. Count me out."

*Count me out*—three words that changed everything.

To be honest, Elijah was too scared to say anything else.

What would happen if Sara Childs and Emma Radson came over? Surely nothing more than a little talking? But what if Tyler started being Tyler? Would they be disgusted by Elijah too? What would he say to convince them he was a good guy?

Elijah decided it was better to just stay home. It wasn't that he didn't like the idea of hanging out with Sara and Emma. But it was a situation fraught with frightening decisions. At home, decisions were already made.

So he stayed home. He stayed up all night writing his story "The Stairway to Despair." When he finished, he felt as if an immense weight had been lifted off his shoulders.

The plot was simple enough. It was the tale of a wealthy telescope maker who lived alone in a house on the edge of a small village. He chose to watch the world from a distance. The only thing he truly cared about was discovering what was hidden behind the clouds that always hung over the village. Since his telescopes couldn't see through the clouds, he paid to have a giant stairway built into the sky. And since he didn't trust what he couldn't see, he asked his neighbors to climb the stairs and place the eye of his biggest telescope on the other side of the clouds. One by one, all the people from the village lugged the giant telescope up the stairs, but once they reached the clouds, one by one they all disappeared.

The telescope maker considered climbing up after them, but thought better of it. He walked into the village instead, and explored the houses of his former neighbors. He went through their drawers, read their diaries, looked closely at their lives. As he learned more about them, he suddenly became interested in them. He couldn't believe it, but he missed them. He rushed back to the stairway, ready to take the risk and join his former neighbors in the sky. It was windy out and, as he approached the first step, the clouds parted for a quick moment, revealing a group of people gathered on a platform at the top of the stairs. Together they pushed, yanked, and pulled the wooden stairs, which heaved and swayed and then started cracking. As they tumbled from the sky, the stairs landed squarely on the telescope maker's house, crushing and shattering all the telescopes inside. Everything was reduced to a pile of wood and glass.

In the last moments of the story, the telescope maker managed to walk away from the rubble. He went back to the village and into a house. He closed all the blinds. He descended to the basement. He vowed never to look up in the sky again.

"It's an interesting allegory," Mrs. Reed told Elijah when he presented the story to her the next day.

"It's meaningful," Elijah insisted, not completely understanding her. "That's what it is."

"What do you say to entering it in a contest?"

A few weeks later, Elijah was more than just a writer. He was an *award-winning* writer. At the same time, Tyler had become more than a seventh-grade boy. He was a seventh-grade boy *with* a girlfriend, and Elijah started to look at his best friend differently. What he'd once seen as a wild sense of humor, he now realized was cruelty. What he'd once seen as rebellion, he now saw as immaturity.

To Elijah, Tyler was a bully, and artists weren't friends with bullies. Tyler's opinion on the matter could be summed up in the one phrase he kept saying when they passed each other in the halls:

"Maybe I should call you Eliza?"

Down in the room, Elijah released his hands from the edge of the bunk. They had stopped shaking.

"If this were a story I was going to write," he said to the others, "someone would have to go back through that hole. He would have to take the risk. Otherwise, he'd always wonder what might have been."

# Chapter 11
# EDDIE

It was 11:30 on Monday night. The lights were out, but Eddie was hunched over his desk. The only glow came from Wendell's watch, a hulking device that was equipped with a calculator, a GPS, and a variety of simple video games.

Elijah sketched lightly with the nub of a pencil on a blank page torn from the back of one of the test books. He was drawing rooms and hallways. He was making Eddie a map.

"Go through it again," Eddie said.

"There are blind spots, under the cameras. Here, here, and here," Bijay said, pointing to spots on the map.

"And I can hide there?" Eddie said.

"Yes," Bijay said. "But to move, you must watch how they pan back and forth. It's outdated technology. Old and slow. And they're only on one side of the wall. If you time it right, you should be able to make it through the halls without ever being detected."

"Ooooh, like Castle Wolfenstein," Wendell said, rocking back and forth with excitement.

"What?" Eddie said.

"It's just a, you know, a classic . . . video ga— Never mind," Wendell said.

"Are they hooked into alarms?" Eddie turned back to Bijay.

"I don't think they are," Bijay said. "I hope they aren't."

"What about the cameras in the rooms?" Eddie asked.

"They're fakes," Bijay said. "Don't let the blinking lights fool you. The school couldn't afford real cameras for every room, so they put in decoys. They think it discourages . . . stuff."

"And they teach you this in AV club?" Elijah said.

"Not the teachers," Bijay said. "Jacob Wade told me."

"Ugh, Jacob," Denton said. "You mean the movie quoter?"

"I can't stand that kid." Eddie groaned. "Everything he says is a stupid movie or TV quote. You know how he greets me in the hall? 'It's not easy being Green.' What a dope."

"A dope who knows a lot about security cameras," Bijay put forth.

Eddie rolled his eyes, then shifted the conversation back to the task at hand. "So I'm safe as long as I'm in a room?" He looked closely at the map, zeroing in on the auditorium, the gym, and other large rooms he could navigate instead of hallways.

"Except for Snodgrass's office," Bijay said. "It's rigged wall to wall with real cameras. No blind spots."

"But that's where I'm going!" Eddie said. "And they're sure to check those DVDs!"

"There's one way," Bijay said. "But you have to move fast."

Eddie smiled. "Fast I can do."

"Between twelve-thirty-seven and twelve-forty-one every night, the DVDs switch over," Bijay explained. "Or they did, last I knew. They'll be off for those four minutes. As long as anything you move gets put back in the exact same place, they probably won't notice."

"Four minutes. If I can run a mile in that time, I can search an office," Eddie said, snatching up the map. "Now or never, right?"

"Leave no stone unturned," Elijah said firmly. "You're a brave kid, Eddie."

"Just find what you can," Denton said. "Good luck and Godspeed."

"Really? Godspeed? They make 'em different there in England, don't they." Eddie laughed as he removed the poster from the wall.

Eddie had to do this alone. No one else could fit through the hole. And even if they could, they probably weren't athletic enough to climb the pipes.

Climbing pipes wasn't too difficult for Eddie, once he got the hang of it. Shinny them like ropes, or take to them like ladders, pushing off from the joints with his feet. Come to a dead end, turn around. Monkey business, really.

He only had to grab one hot pipe before he knew to tap every following pipe and make sure they were cool. The main problem (and this was a big one): he had no idea where he would end up.

To his forehead, Eddie had strapped Wendell's watch, which was held tight with a headband made from the handle of the plastic bag Snodgrass had left behind. The GPS did him little good, but the watch's eerie glow was enough to let him see a few feet in front of him. He was essentially in a cave, pawing at walls and pulling himself through passageways, striving to find some pockets of light.

As terrifying as it all was, there was one thing Eddie knew he had to do: keep moving. The sooner he found his way out, the more time he had to explore the school.

"Please, no growling," Eddie whispered to himself as he scurried through the dark. "That's all I'm asking."

After about fifteen minutes of climbing, squeezing through tight spots, and retracing his path, he saw a faint glow above him. Drawing closer, he realized it was a small grating letting in shafts of light. He propped himself on a ledge beside it.

He was tempted to kick the grating out, but he had no idea where it might land. Luckily, there were nuts and bolts to remove. He twisted the nuts free, then wove his fingers through the grating, eased it forward, turned it, and pulled it back through the opening. He stuck his head out to see where he was.

Tiny lights from above provided a faint illumination. It

was about a ten-foot drop to the floor below. Turning his head around, he nearly hit his nose on the ceiling. He could see a hallway extending on either side of him, and could just make out the cameras staggered and mounted on the opposite wall. They were panning back and forth.

He paused a moment, pondering his next move. He noticed the cameras were mounted slightly below the level of the grating. They were tilted on a gentle downward angle.

They can't see me, he told himself as he eased his feet out from the opening and rocked back and forth, gathering momentum. Before his mind could process the consequences, he was launching himself through the air and landing in a crumpled heap in the dead center of the hall, like a bird on a pane of glass.

It was a stupid move.

And as he hopped to his feet, he locked eyes with one of the cameras.

He had no choice but to sprint right for it until he was safely beneath it. He pressed his aching body against the wall and took a deep breath.

It's all over, he thought. Spotted! As fast as that. An alarm has been triggered. McKenzie is on his way. Their only escape route will be found.

Even if there was no alarm, Eddie knew he was being recorded. His face, his eyes. Clear as day. Snodgrass will check it. He'll come for me, Eddie thought. He'll punish me in ways I can't even imagine.

Now, instinct demanded that he run. Run to the nearest exit. Go home. Climb into his own bed. Forget about the others. Forget about what his parents might know. Hide under his covers and just hope it all went away. But he was paralyzed for the first time in his life. He pressed himself flatter against the wall and closed his eyes.

He wondered what the others were doing. Were they asleep? Probably not. They were probably waiting for him to return. They were counting on him. One thing they certainly weren't doing was calling him a spaz. He might not have been a hero to them, but he was someone they trusted. Now he had gone and let them down.

He waited for what seemed like an eternity. There was no other movement in the hall—no alarms, no indication that he had been detected.

He opened his eyes and looked up at the camera above him. It panned slowly back and forth. There was something wrong with it, though. A frayed wire stuck out from the back. Could it be broken? Blind? He had no way of knowing, but there was a chance. He'd take that chance.

Eddie drew in a deep breath and felt a rush of adrenaline dance through his body. So I won't get an A-plus in cat burglary, he thought. It doesn't mean I should give up. The race isn't over until you cross the finish line.

He could see another camera farther down the hall, sweeping back and forth. Eddie realized that by timing things right, just as Bijay had said, he could move along the wall without any of the cameras detecting him.

Pressed firmly to the tiles, Eddie slid slowly along, watching the cameras and timing his movements accordingly. Before long, he was beneath the next camera. Then he started the process all over again—watching, sliding, taking things slow.

Once he reached the third camera, he was steps away from the door to the cafeteria. He waited, made his move, slipped inside.

It was dark in the cafeteria, but from what Eddie could see, it was completely different from how he remembered it. All the artwork and nutritional posters had been removed from the walls. It was no longer populated with the round yellow tables he had eaten at for the past couple of years. Instead, there were two parallel rows of long, sturdy black tables, lined with plastic ketchup and mustard bottles. On the wall at one end of the tables was a giant sign:

# IDAHO TESTS! FOOD FOR YOUR MIND!

On the opposite wall was an image he knew well. He'd seen it on television, on billboards, even tattooed on the bicep of a guy who worked at the local convenience store.

It was a giant pickle. The pickle had a face and feet and hands, and was wearing a baseball cap sideways. One hand was giving the thumbs-up; the other was pointing directly down at the tables. A banner above the pickle read:

## Join the Mackers Revolution!

Over twenty feet tall, it was not just any pickle. It was Peter Pickle, the official "spokespickle" for Mackers.

Taking another step inside, Eddie heard a crinkling sound at his feet. He looked down to discover the floor was a sea of burger and fry wrappers. Trash cans were overflowing; paper and cardboard were strewn everywhere.

There might have been an unbearable stink to it, if it all hadn't been picked clean. The evidence of a feeding frenzy was all around him, but there was no sign of actual food.

Eddie waded through the ankle-deep garbage to the opposite corner of the cafeteria. Snodgrass's office was nearby. That was his destination. The cafeteria in all its strangeness was of little importance. He opened the nearest door.

Standing beneath another camera, Eddie removed his headband and checked the watch: 12:36. The door to Snodgrass's office was just a few steps away. He couldn't believe their plan was actually working. He watched the camera. He watched the watch. He watched the camera: 12:37. He went for it.

Inside the office, there was bound to be something that would prove their innocence. That was the hope, at least.

But all hope was lost when he reached the door. As he grabbed the knob and tried to give it a twist, nothing budged. It was locked.

How had they not thought of that? They had figured out pipes and security cameras and everything else but had forgotten about simple locks. Eddie tugged on the door for a few moments, then scrambled back under the camera. He didn't know how to pick locks. Surely it wasn't as easy as it seemed on television.

When the camera panned away again, he slid back over to the door. He gave it another tug, then scanned the edges, looking for a hidden key or a place to remove the hinges. Eddie might have been a troublemaker, but he wasn't a criminal. Breaking and entering was new to him.

What he found was a small panel on the wall, just

below the knob. He pried it open to reveal a keypad, almost identical to the one that operated the door to their cell. He was tempted to try his luck with it, but had no idea what might happen if he typed in the wrong code. As the camera swung back in his direction, he shut the panel and slid back to safety.

"Stupid friggin' . . . ," Eddie growled. He scraped his fingernails against the wall behind him, trying to liberate some energy. He had a distinct desire to bite something. He put his forearm in his mouth and clenched down his teeth. It hurt, but it also calmed him down.

He closed his eyes and tried to think things through. To get into Snodgrass's office, they would need a better plan. His only option at this point was to go back. But how on earth was he going to climb back up through the grating in the hall? It was ten feet high!

That was when he heard the footsteps. They sounded like tap-dancing, a frenzy of feet going *pitter-pat, pitter-pat, pitter-pat, pitter-pat*.

Then silence. Then a frenzy of feet again, louder and closer than before. Then silence.

Eddie's eyelids snapped open. He saw a mass of darkness at the other end of the hall. Was it a shadow? Or something else? All he could tell was that it was coming toward him.

The camera panned and Eddie moved away from the shape as quickly as he could. He prayed that he wouldn't hear that rumbling growl.

Eddie had watched enough nature documentaries to know which animals he could beat in a race.

A snake: six-minute mile.

An elephant: five-minute mile.

Eddie: four-and-a-half-minute mile.

A cheetah: one-minute mile.

The cheetah was the fastest animal on land. The question now was, what was the fastest animal in the school?

*Pitter-pat, pitter-pat, pitter-pat, pitter-pat.*

Eddie turned the corner and faced another long hallway. He assessed the cameras and continued on. When he had reached the halfway point, the dark mass appeared around the corner. It was following directly in his path.

He grabbed the latch to the first door he came upon. It was tight at first, so he put his entire body into it. When the latch finally turned, the door opened and he tumbled into a dark corner of the library.

Eddie jumped to his feet, closed the door, and clumsily attached the watch back to his forehead. He didn't exactly have intimate knowledge of the library. His brain was a database of facts drawn from television and the Internet. Why waste time cracking a book when a Google search or a click of the remote could feed his mind? Sure, he'd been in the library before, but the only thing he knew was there would be plenty of books to hide behind, no cameras to deal with, and now his speed was back in play.

He began to run. Though when he looked from side to side, he noticed something extremely strange: there were no books in the library. The shelves were bare. Nothing but dust bunnies. It was as if a plague had swept through.

Then he heard the footsteps again. The chase was back on. Eddie quickened his pace, weaving through the empty shelves, past tables, and over and around any obstacle in his way.

Yet somehow, he was losing the race. His pursuer was gaining on him. There was no one in the school, and only a few people in the whole state, who could actually catch Eddie. Still, the footsteps were getting closer while Eddie was running as fast as he possibly could.

Up a flight of stairs, through row after row of shelves, he kept sprinting, too scared to look behind him. And the footsteps kept coming.

Where to turn? Where to hide? Without any books, the library felt as wide open as a gymnasium. And when, through the glow of the watch, Eddie found himself facing a corner, his only choice was to turn around.

The footsteps slowed to a jog, and a figure emerged in the dim light. Bone white teeth. A wide grin. It stepped closer as Eddie cowered in the corner. For a moment, he thought of putting his hand over the watch, closing his eyes, and letting it all end in the darkness. Instead, he decided to face his fate.

# Chapter 12

# DENTON

The hour was ungodly. The room was pitch-black. Their voices were soft. And Denton couldn't believe Eddie wasn't back yet.

"Have you?" Wendell asked Elijah.

"I was gonna say sort of, but actually . . . no. Not yet," Elijah said.

"How about you, B?" Wendell asked.

"Oh no, not even close," Bijay said.

"Denton?"

"Well . . ." Denton hesitated for a moment. He was sure telling the truth would make them jealous. Then again, it was something he was reasonably proud of. So he finally said, "Yes. I have."

"Really?" Wendell said. "What was it like?"

"It was perfectly pleasant."

"You kissed a girl and all you can say is that it was pleasant?" Elijah laughed.

"*Perfectly* pleasant," Denton reiterated. "You can't get any more pleasant than that."

"Did you use your tongue?" Bijay asked.

"Yes, I suppose I did. At least a tad."

"And was this girl imaginary?" Elijah asked.

"No, as a matter of fact, she was from Scotland."

"Scotland is like England's Canada, isn't it?" Elijah teased. "That imaginary land to the north."

"If you must know, we met in the Cotswolds."

"Is that one of those wizard schools?" Bijay asked.

"Yes, Bijay. We met at wizard school."

"See, Elijah," Bijay said, "she *is* imaginary. Even I know there's no such thing as wizard school."

"You know who I've always wanted to kiss?" Elijah said. "Carla Rossi."

"Best of luck with that." Denton chortled. "Chad Mitchum would snap your skinny neck."

"Okay, Jude Law," Elijah shot back. "Who've you got your eye on?"

"If I had to choose? I suppose Karen Esposito isn't horrible," Denton said.

"Yeah, not horrible," Wendell said. "Just gorgeous."

Denton wasn't about to tell them, but he thought Karen Esposito was more than gorgeous. She was perfection.

Thirteen years old, yet not a trace of acne. Her hair was dark and straight and long, and Denton loved to sit behind her in social studies and just stare into its velvety blackness. It smelled liked the beach. Her eyes were an alluring green, which people said were the result of tinted contacts. Her voice was calm and crisp, a singer's voice.

Denton knew that maintaining such an image must take a lot of time. To him, it showed an admirable amount of determination. It couldn't leave much room for schoolwork. Still, he had heard that Karen scored consistent Bs.

She was nice to everyone. She smiled to people in the hall, actually made eye contact. She remembered names. She seemed to have no secrets, no demons, no insecurities. She was completely up-front about who she was and what it took to be her.

Denton noticed that the school reacted to her in one of two ways. Boys would blush and stutter in her presence. Girls would chat politely with her, but as soon as she was out of earshot, they would whisper suspiciously among themselves.

Denton figured they were just jealous. He knew what it felt like to be misunderstood. Denton and Karen worked hard to look the way they did. If others couldn't achieve the same results, it was because they weren't trying hard enough. They were kindred spirits, he and Karen. Made for each other.

There was one catch. Denton had never said a word to her.

"Esposito," Elijah scoffed. "She's only interested in high

school lacrosse players, you know? You don't even have a clue what lacrosse is, do you?"

"With the sticks? Silly game with a French name? Please," Denton quipped. He'd seen lacrosse before, but no, he didn't have a clue how it was played. Another oddity of America.

"Who's your girl, Wen?" Elijah asked.

Wendell paused. His face grew flushed. "I'll tell you who I hate," he finally said. "Sally Dibbs."

"Who's Sally Dibbs?" Denton asked.

"New girl," Wendell said with a huff. "Rides my bus. Asks the stupidest questions."

"There are no stupid questions," Bijay said sincerely.

"Only stupid people," Elijah and Denton said at the same time. They locked eyes for a second. No one called jinx. Sharing a point of view with Elijah wasn't exactly something Denton valued. Elijah was recklessly rebellious, while Denton relied on logic.

Elijah turned away first. "So, you hate Sally Dibbs," he said to Wendell. "Then who do you . . . you know?"

Wendell paused again. "It's personal, all right."

His tone was a bit too defensive. Denton feared that Wendell might have another episode. If he could put a hole in a wall, he could probably do a lot worse.

"How about you, Bijay," Denton asked, shifting the focus. "Who do you want to kiss?"

"I don't know," Bijay said. "Anyone, I guess."

"Right on," Elijah said. "With an attitude like that, you'll do fine."

Right then PERSEVERANCE started to glow. Just a pinprick at first; then, like a stain spreading over fabric, light enveloped the entire poster. It was an encouraging sign. It had been hours since Eddie had left.

Bijay rose from his bunk and walked over to the poster. "Finally," he said as he carefully pulled it down.

Denton sat up from his bunk. Through the hole, he saw the glowing watch first, dead center on someone's forehead. Only the forehead wasn't Eddie's—bangs now hung over the watch. Denton gulped as he looked down into the person's eyes.

"You!" Bijay screamed, jumping away.

"Me!" said Tyler Kelly, smiling back at them.

"Eddie's mutated!" Bijay screamed. "He's become Tyler Kelly! Hit the button! Wake McKenzie!"

"Don't wake McKenzie," Eddie said, appearing alongside Tyler. "Everything's fine."

Nudging Tyler out of the way, Eddie thrust his arms and head up through the hole. As Denton backed away, Wendell came over and grabbed Eddie's hands and started pulling.

"Give me a push, buddy," Eddie said to Tyler.

"Sure thing," Tyler said.

With the extra help, Eddie passed through the hole with relative ease.

"A big thanks, Ty," Eddie said.

"You are most welcome, Edward," Tyler said.

"Where on earth were you?" Denton asked like a scolding parent. "And where on earth did you find him? And why on earth would you bring him here?"

"He was in the library," Eddie said. "He was looking for books."

"They say that reading is *fun*damental," Tyler said with an odd amount of enthusiasm. "It's far more than just a pun, you know. It's fun and addicting and fulfilling and gives your brain a case of the warm fuzzies. I adore reading! I read all the books in my house this evening. So I thought, Perhaps I'll visit the school and see what's left in the library. I had heard there had been a run on books, but good heavens. Not a single volume left."

"And he saw me," Eddie explained. "So he chased me down to say hello."

"A cordial 'how do you do' between friends," Tyler said, staring straight ahead.

Denton stared straight back at Tyler. There was something different about his eyes. They were distant. They were spiritless.

"Okay, this is more than a bit weird," Elijah said. "Does anyone else find this weird?"

"Yeah, Tyler, why aren't you teasing us?" Wendell said. "Or punching us?"

"That's humorous," Tyler said with a manufactured giggle. "You're quite humorous, Wendell. I never knew that about you. But then, we never had much of a chance to get to know each other before, did we?"

"I guess not," Wendell said cautiously.

"You really missed a wonderful day of school," Tyler said. "Everyone is studying hard, as they should. We have the pep rally on Thursday. Boy, do I love pep. And the food . . . the food is absolutely splendid."

"Mackers?" Bijay asked, leaning in to hear more.

Tyler's eyes rolled back. Drool began to collect on his

lips. He licked it back up far too enthusiastically. "Double Double Triple," he moaned.

Denton wasn't completely immune to the lure of fast food, but he had never seen such a gluttonous display. It was appalling. And obviously, Denton wasn't alone in his feelings.

"Okay, now you're *really* freakin' us out, Tyler," Elijah said.

"All apologies," Tyler said, his eyes scrolling back to attention. "I find myself getting carried away sometimes. Edward told me you were down here on a secret mission. I shouldn't be a bother much longer. I shall retain your confidence and return home."

"What else can you tell us?" Denton asked. He wasn't entirely fooled by this new version of Tyler. It had to be some sort of act. The more Denton got him talking, the more chances Tyler would have to slip up and reveal his true agenda. It was a classic legal maneuver: keep the witness on the stand.

"He can't tell us much," Eddie jumped in. "I asked him everything I could think of. Doesn't know a thing about Snodgrass. All he talks about is studying and eating."

"Two of life's greatest pleasures," Tyler said. "Wouldn't you agree?"

"Sure." Eddie reached forward and pulled the watch off Tyler's head. He checked the time. "It'll be morning soon. McKenzie will be here. You should get going."

"Agreed," Tyler said.

"Will you be able to make it in the dark?" Eddie asked.

"Of course," Tyler said. "You were a fine navigator, and I made a mental map of the pipes on the way down. Who needs eyes when you've got your mind? All I have to do is count the joints, calculate the distance, and I'll be back in the school in no time. Dodge some cameras. Slip back through the window. Scurry home. Simple stuff."

"Simple stuff indeed," Denton said suspiciously.

But before he could get another word in, he heard Tyler leaping onto the pipes and starting to climb. Denton grabbed the watch from Eddie, put his head through the hole, and held the watch up. In the weak light, he could see Tyler scrambling like a squirrel from pipe to pipe until he disappeared into the darkness.

# Chapter 13

# ELIJAH

The situation was now worse than Elijah could have imagined. As he lay in his bunk on Tuesday morning, he kept thinking about Tyler. Denton had insisted Tyler was putting them on, but Elijah knew Tyler wasn't that talented an actor. While he loved to mess with people's heads, he always struck immediately. He never left a room without letting you know who was in control.

Last night, there had been no punchline. No punch, even. Nothing resembling the real Tyler. It was scary.

Eddie's description of the school only worried Elijah more. They had missed only a day and a half, but it sounded as though the entire place had been transformed. Fast-food trash everywhere. A library purged of books. It was the stuff of bad dreams.

It took McKenzie's arrival with breakfast to make Elijah rise from bed.

"Halfway there," McKenzie said with a smile. "Not an easy feat. Keep at it."

With each day, the coach seemed to ease up on them a little. Elijah assumed he must have known more than he was letting on. Maybe they were going to be down there longer than Snodgrass had told them, and McKenzie just didn't see the point in destroying their self-esteem anymore. Elijah had seen a television show once about prisoners on death row. The guards often treated them better than all the other inmates.

This scared him too.

No one else was sure what the next step should be, either. Over breakfast, they discussed their options in low whispers.

"We could be trapped here forever," Elijah said, sniffing at his glass of cranberry juice. He placed it down, deciding against it.

"We need hard evidence," Denton said.

"What we need is Nurse Bloom to come back," Wendell said.

It was like summoning a genie. Almost as soon as the words came out of Wendell's mouth, the door opened slowly and Nurse Bloom walked in.

Her eyes were washed-out and pink. Elijah wouldn't have described her as haggard, but she looked run-down, exhausted. Beneath her white coat, she wore a wool turtleneck sweater, an odd choice for the middle of spring.

She closed the door and smiled reassuringly.

"Nurse Bloom. Thank God," Wendell said tenderly.

But Elijah wasn't as easily swayed. He watched anxiously as she patted Wendell on the head. Then she pinched one of his hairs between her thumb and forefinger and plucked it.

Wendell winced but didn't say a thing. She patted him on the head again, as if it were her best try at an apology. Then she produced a plastic bag from inside her jacket and carefully dropped the hair into it. A piece of masking tape was stuck to the bottom edge of the bag. In black marker on the tape, someone had written *Wendell Scoop*.

In a swift movement, Nurse Bloom was standing above Elijah. Before he could object, she plucked a hair from his scalp and dropped it into another plastic bag. She quickly moved on.

As she plucked the hairs from Denton's, Eddie's and Bijay's heads, they each greeted her with befuddled stares.

She was a nurse, so she was careful, and it didn't seem to hurt anyone. She was also a woman, and if Elijah's sister was any indication, then he knew that women did strange things. It was nothing, really, just a hair off their heads. Yet it felt like some sort of betrayal.

Finally, she stopped next to Wendell and reached into her jacket. This time she pulled out an envelope. As she handed it to him, her sleeve drew back from her hand, revealing her wrist. Splotchy and red, the skin looked burned, as if it had been plunged into boiling water.

"Open it when you're ready," she said softly.

"Nurse Bloom," Wendell said with concern, "are you . . . ?"

She simply smiled again and pulled her hand away. "Goodbye," she said. Then she opened the door and Snodgrass stepped inside.

"Well done, Nora," he said. "You may go now."

"Thank you, Lionel." Nurse Bloom hung her head and slinked out of the room.

"Gentlemen," Snodgrass said. "I trust you missed me."

Elijah had gotten used to not seeing Snodgrass. He felt his lip twisting up in disgust, so he grabbed his test book and looked at it instead.

"Glad you're enjoying your test books, but we're gonna have a study break." He held a cell phone up in the air for all to see.

"Do we get to order pizza?" Eddie asked.

"Not your best material, Mr. Green," Snodgrass said. "No pizza today. Only calls home."

Snodgrass removed a handful of folded papers from his pocket. "On Sunday, you'll be happy to know, you all e-mailed your parents," Snodgrass went on. "Lovely messages, all sent from your school accounts. I love you, I miss you, so on and so forth. The writing was top-notch."

He sorted through the papers and then handed one to each of them.

"Now you will leave these messages on your parents' voice mails," he said.

"We can't speak to them?" Denton asked.

"They're not home," Snodgrass said.

"And how do you know that?" Elijah snapped back. Snodgrass's confidence was maddening. Somehow, he had to prove him wrong.

"Because I already called, Mr. Rosen," Snodgrass said. "It is a workday, after all. Please give me some credit. Some of us think things through."

Wendell looked puzzled by his paper. "Mine says 'Montreal is off the hook' and 'Mensa is the dopest.' Who talks like that?"

"Kids talk like that," Snodgrass said firmly.

"No, we don't," Elijah said with a smirk.

"You have me saying 'Cheerio!' at the end of mine," Denton said.

"He at least got that right. You do say things like that," Eddie said.

"I'd never say cheerio!" Denton protested.

"Fine," Snodgrass said, snatching the papers from their hands. "Forget the scripts. Just say that you're having a wonderful time. That Coach McKenzie is an excellent chaperone. That you're sorry you haven't been able to call home sooner."

"What if we don't want to?" Elijah said defiantly.

"Well, let's see," Snodgrass said. "There's the matter of the evidence. Still the issue of some stolen money."

"You know we didn't steal that money." Elijah stood up. "So let's just say we let the cat out of the bag right now. Tell them where we are. You can bring in the police. Show them your evidence. We'll roll the dice, as they say."

Wendell reached out to grab Elijah's shoulder, but he brushed him off. Forget all this cloak-and-dagger bull. All he wanted to do was go home. Snodgrass, for all his talk, was not infallible.

"You go ahead and roll the dice, *as they say,*" Snodgrass snarled, "because the dice are rigged. You think I haven't planned for such foolishness? You know who'll suffer the most? Your precious little pal Nurse Bloom. You don't think I know she's made you promises she can't keep? Let me tell you something about her. She's a coward."

"Not a chance," Wendell said.

"She was hired for two reasons—her long legs," Snodgrass said. "Your honorable Principal Phipps fell for her, and fell hard. Didn't think with his brain. Thought like a thirteen-year-old boy. She's not even a registered nurse, just a pretty face who couldn't hack it in grad school. Why do you think Phipps left? I was ready to expose her."

"Lies," Wendell whimpered. Elijah nodded in support.

"I'm working to turn this school around," Snodgrass went on. "And she is just in the way. When you finally leave this room, you'll see what I mean. This school is taking things to the next level. And Nurse Bloom is not part of its future. She's just looking out for herself, following orders, and hoping that I let her off the hook."

"We don't believe you. It's our word against yours," Elijah said. He was trying to sound defiant, but his confidence was wavering and his voice was shaky.

"Really?" Snodgrass smiled, seeming to sense Elijah's fear. "There's no evidence I've ever even been down here. Have you seen me touch anything? Bloom, her fingerprints are everywhere. Her hair is scattered throughout this room. So it's *my* word against *hers*. And when the world learns the other lies she's been weaving, who do you think they'll believe? Vice Principal Snodgrass, the educator with the immaculate record who assumes his five best students have been called away to Montreal? Or Nurse Bloom, the dishonest, raven-haired liar who employs young boys to steal money for her, then shelters the juvenile delinquents in a secret room beneath the school?"

"What about McKenzie?" Denton pressed. A good point, Elijah thought. Snodgrass hadn't covered all his bases.

"McKenzie?" Snodgrass chuckled. "He's like all soldiers. Easily manipulated. Easily quieted. Disposable."

Elijah wanted to scream, but his body wouldn't let him. His throat was heaving and his stomach turning. He couldn't make a sound. He could only sit back down.

"You know what?" Snodgrass smiled, holding the cell phone back up. "I even borrowed Ms. Bloom's phone. You're first, Mr. Rosen."

Snodgrass pressed the Send button on the phone, then tossed it to Elijah. He caught it and held it in his lap, staring at it as the call connected. After the fifth ring, he heard his mother's voice on an electronic recording.

*"You've reached the Rosens. If you have a message for Debby, Mike, Tara, Elijah, or even Puddles, leave it at the beep. Thanks!"*

The sound of her voice cut deep. Man, did he miss his family. With everything Snodgrass had said, with everything they had speculated about, it was impossible to know what to believe.

Elijah slowly raised the phone to his ear. Rather than make something up or try to send some covert message, he just found himself saying what he was feeling.

"Hi, everyone," he said softly. "It's me. I feel so far away from you all right now. But that's natural, I guess . . . when you're away from home. I'm doing fine. I'm learning a lot. The people here are nice and real smart. It's tough, though. So I'm glad I'll be home soon. I miss you all, especially Puddles. And I love you all . . . so much."

Snodgrass began clapping. "Well done. I knew you had it in you. All of you do. But *Puddles,* Mr. Rosen? A pooch should have a more robust name, don't you think? My dog, Xerxes, for instance, is a canine of the highest order."

"Duly noted," Elijah grumbled as he handed the phone over.

"Just a piece of advice," Snodgrass huffed. "And as for the rest of you, I want you to follow Mr. Rosen's lead. Do as I say, and everything will work out in the end. For you, for Ms. Bloom, for all of Ho-Ho-Kus."

Elijah watched with dismay as the others made the same call and left nearly identical messages. When they were finished, Snodgrass, beaming from yet another victory, stepped into the doorway.

"Only a few days left, gentlemen. Keep to your books and I will keep my word."

"What a liar," Wendell said when Snodgrass was gone. "Nurse Bloom always comes through."

He tore open the envelope Nurse Bloom had given him and pulled out a sheet of paper. Almost immediately, his face sank.

"What's it say?" Eddie asked.

"She knows I like Sudoku," Wendell said with

disappointment, showing them the page. "I guess she's worried about us . . . getting bored."

That was all the page was: a Sudoku puzzle. A few numbers were filled in to get things started. Elijah had never really done a Sudoku puzzle before. He knew it had something to do with putting numbers into boxes. The only thing that seemed to distinguish this one was a message scrawled in pen at the top. It read:

Solutions to our problems? True heroes employ patience. Every puzzle requires abilities life leaves you.

"What could that mean?" Eddie asked.

"Nonsense," Denton said. "She's off her nut."

Denton is right, Elijah thought. It was becoming apparent that they could no longer rely on Nurse Bloom. Snodgrass's promises were a joke. Who on the outside was going to help them?

Nobody. That was one thing Elijah was sure about. If they were going to get out of there, they were going to have to act on their own.

Then it came to him.

"Computer hacking, that's sort of like doing puzzles, right?" Elijah asked Wendell.

"Sorta," Wendell said, folding up the puzzle and placing it in his pocket.

"If Eddie could get you the parts, could you build a computer?" Elijah asked him.

"Maybe." Wendell shrugged.

"Then you can hack in and control the whole school?" Bijay said excitedly. "Like in the movies?"

"Not exactly," Wendell said. "But, theoretically, I could probably disable some alarms. I could access some information. Files, manuals, that kinda stuff."

"Passwords? Combinations? E-mails?" Elijah said.

"I dunno, I guess," Wendell said.

Ideas were piling on top of each other in Elijah's head. It was like writing a story. When inspiration struck, Elijah grabbed onto an idea and let it take him wherever it led.

*A computer*. That was the idea he focused on now. It was a starting point, a link to the outside world. It would give them information, and information was power. What they would do with that power was hard to say. But they had to do something.

"Guys," Elijah said. "It's time to take some bigger risks."

# Chapter 14
# WENDELL

"In the back of the computer lab, there's a closet full of old parts," Wendell told Eddie. "No one's gonna notice if some of it's missing. Bring back as much stuff as you can carry."

Eddie was game. They waited until after dinner; then they tied bedsheets around him like a tunic. He was to use them as ropes, or bags, or whatever he needed, if he found himself in a pinch. Then Wendell strapped the watch to Eddie's head and they sent him on his way.

A computer! Its hum and glow, that was what Wendell was looking forward to most. Even without games, it was something familiar. It was like inviting an old friend into the room with them.

Eddie returned less than thirty minutes later, confidence pulsing through his face. "I think I'm getting the hang of this," he said. "There are shortcuts everywhere in this place."

Over his shoulder, he carried a sheet tied in a bundle. Inside was a smorgasbord of computer parts—wires, hard drives, keypads, discs, modems, the works. He even brought back wire-cutters and a set of mini-screwdrivers. He fed it all back through the hole, or at least what could fit through it.

"What are we supposed to do with this screen?" Eddie said, trying and failing to push it through.

"I guess we'll just have to leave it back there," Wendell said. "We can still hook it up. You'll just have to prop it up somewhere, and I'll have to do my work with my head in the hole."

"Whatever it takes, right?" Eddie said.

Wendell got to work, splicing wires and moving around chips and circuit boards. He cursed and sweated and kept at it. He could feel the others watching him quietly over his shoulder, but no one said a word—until Eddie casually remarked, "I think there's something going on up there."

Wendell paused.

"What do you mean, something going on?" Denton said.

"In the school. Like a meeting or something? There are people in the halls. Adults."

"Well, get up there and see what it is!" Elijah said excitedly.

"Really," Eddie said, "should I?"

Denton paused. Then he said, "If you think you can do it without being seen, I don't see why not."

"Wendell?" Eddie asked. "You're cool?"

Wendell slugged back some bottled water. There was nothing he wanted more than to get back to his pile of electronics. For the last few days, he had felt useless. But now . . .

"I'm good," Wendell said, smiling for the first time in days. "I'm great, actually. I've got a lot of work to do. Take your time. Eat some Mackers while you're out."

"And be careful," Denton added.

Eddie was back through the hole in seconds.

It took Wendell barely an hour. The results were hardly pretty. It was a mess of wires and circuit boards, a bulky rounded screen, disc drives and reconfigured modems, and all manner of equipment that most people would have relegated to the trash ten years ago.

Still, beauty had nothing to do with function, and Wendell was pretty sure it would work.

He handed a cord to Bijay, who crouched next to an outlet in the wall and inserted the plug. "Ready to go," he said.

Gingerly, Wendell used a pencil eraser to press a node on a circuit board. He took a step back and all four boys looked through the hole at the screen, which was sitting behind the wall atop all their test books. A green dot appeared in the middle of it and expanded slowly, like a ripple in water. Then the screen went completely black.

"Oh, man," Elijah said disappointedly.

"Just give it a second," Wendell said cautiously. And just when he was ready to give up hope, a blinking green cursor appeared at the bottom of the screen. "Nice!" Wendell cheered.

Denton leaned in so close, his nose almost touched the screen. "That's it," he said. "Where are the folders? The programs? The desktop wallpaper?"

"A lot of the parts I used were old," Wendell said. "It's a DOS system."

"What's a DOS?" Bijay said.

"DOS, well, DOS is old. Older than us." It was the best way Wendell could explain things. He had found that once he started talking programming to people who didn't know a thing about it, he ended up confusing them even more.

"Can I check my Facebook page?" Bijay asked. "I installed a new application called Bollyweird. It lets you follow all the latest gossip from Mumbai."

"How about my Gmail?" Denton asked. "Maybe if we sent a message to someone we trusted—"

"Yeah, and there's this hilarious thing on YouTube that you guys gotta see where a guinea pig chases a Rottweiler," Bijay said.

"It's not like that." Wendell sighed. "It's only green. It's only text. No graphics. No sound. Almost no memory."

"This is a computer you're talking about, right?" Elijah asked.

"Of course," Wendell said. "It's just . . . back to the basics."

"So, what are you going to do with it?" Elijah asked.

"I did manage to modify a wireless router, attach it to a newer but slightly damaged motherboard, and then adapt it so . . ." His comments were met with blank stares. "Well, let's just say that assuming I can get a signal, I might be able to tap into the school's intranet," he finished.

"And how hard will that be?" Denton said.

"Next to impossible," Wendell said.

"How long will impossible take?" Elijah asked.

"Who knows?" Wendell shrugged. "Time me."

He pulled a chair up to the wall, placed the keyboard in his lap, and leaned his head into the hole. Then he attacked the keys like a concert pianist, his fingers clacking out a staccato rhythm. Strings of green numbers and letters ate away at the black of the computer screen. His pulse quickened, but he felt calm. His ears went deaf. His back was bent nearly double, but it didn't hurt. His body would not get in the way of his mission.

It didn't feel much different from being at home. Sure, at home he didn't have to stick his head in a hole to see his computer screen, and he never had three other people looking on. But sitting in the dark staring at programming code was how he spent many evenings and weekends.

The irony wasn't lost on Wendell. He was doing this so that he could leave one locked room, only to go home and lock himself in another. Or at least, that was how it used to be. Maybe life would be different when they finally got out.

The night before, Bijay had said they should all hang out together once this whole ordeal was over. Would that really happen? Wendell wasn't so sure.

Denton would probably always think of him as sloppy and clumsy. He assumed Elijah would despise the fact that he enjoyed all the hit songs on the radio and laughed at movies with fart jokes. He knew that Eddie would tease him constantly. And Bijay? Bijay was too nice. Wendell would only manage to disappoint him, just as he seemed to disappoint anyone who relied on him.

Still, he cycled through computer code, trying to find a way into the school's network. He wanted to do his part, because no matter what these guys thought of him, he liked them. They were everything Wendell wasn't. They were charming and funny and creative and outspoken. And down in that room, they were his friends.

So he worked frantically, trying anything he could think of to gain access to the system. And he nearly gasped when he launched a small program he had just created. The screen went black, then green text appeared, blinking hope into the room.

```
USER NAME:
PASSWORD:
```

# Chapter 15

# EDDIE

In the shadows above the lights, high in the rafters near the ceiling, Eddie lay facedown on the steel catwalk watching the school's auditorium fill up with adults.

Eddie recognized the parents of a few friends, but the crowd was too dense to spot his own. There were more than a thousand seats, and people jockeyed to find an open spot. Soon, every chair was occupied. Even more people poured in. They stood wherever they could—in the back, in the aisles, even on the edge of the stage itself. This seemed to be the hottest ticket in town.

When the room was at full capacity, the houselights

lowered and the loud chatter turned to whispers. A solitary spotlight hit the stage, and almost everyone fell silent.

The clack of high heels filled the room. Then Mrs. Kass, the school's secretary, stepped into the spotlight and up to a microphone.

"Good evening, parents," she said enthusiastically. "And thank you for attending this very special meeting of the PTA. I see a lot of familiar faces out there. I see a lot of faces in general! It's quite a turnout, and we are *thrilled* about that. It's an exciting time of year at Ho-Ho-Kus Junior High, and I know some parents have come with concerns. Others have come to show their appreciation for the teachers and staff and all their hard work. There will be ample time to answer questions and talk about your wonderful children. But first we're going to hand the reins over to a man who sees your favorite guys and gals nearly every day. Our good friend and vice principal . . . Lionel Snodgrass!"

Polite applause and a few whistles floated through the auditorium as Mrs. Kass stepped to the side. Then came the sound of large shoes, the heavy thump of rubber on wood.

When Snodgrass stopped at center stage, Eddie felt something he didn't expect—awe. Snodgrass suddenly appeared larger than Eddie remembered, as if the vice principal filled the entire spotlight. When he seized the microphone, he seized the audience. Quite simply, he owned the stage. And Eddie definitely didn't expect to hear what came next.

"Let me tell you about five boys who attend this school," Snodgrass said in a calming, confident tone. "Five fine young *men,* each one talented in his own way. One a competitor. One a wordsmith. One a negotiator. One a performer. One a technician. So often at this stage in life, children are commended for their clothes or their haircuts or their possessions. In the hallways, kids rarely talk about the heart and the mind. Well, these guys have both, in spades. And for a long time, no one seemed to notice.

"A couple of weeks ago, I received a phone call. A very selective organization had caught wind of our geniuses. I'm not afraid to use that word, because that's what they are—*geniuses.* And because our geniuses have showed such strength of character, they were asked to attend a very selective and very secretive conference. Now, I don't want to spill all the beans, but on Friday, they left on a surprise trip that is bound to change those young hearts and minds forever. Your own children often read about rites of passage in their English classes. These five boys are actually living one.

"We are all extremely proud of them. In addition, we are all extremely thankful for the folks who raised them. For while we would love to take all the credit here at Ho-Ho-Kus Junior, it is at home that they learned to be the men they are. I'd like the families of Denton Kensington, Wendell Scoop, Eddie Green, Elijah Rosen, and Bijay Bharata to stand."

Eddie's eyes scanned the masses as couples popped up from their seats. His parents were the fourth couple to rise. From his perch on the catwalk, he couldn't make out their faces, but he assumed they were slightly embarrassed. There was nothing they liked better than championing his accomplishments, but the Old Boy hated being the center of attention.

The crowd honored all the families with a hearty round of applause. Eddie assumed the other boys would ask him later about their families; he would say they all looked fantastic. It wouldn't be a lie so much as an assumption, because his eyes wouldn't budge from his own parents.

"As these parents take their seats, I want to thank them one more time," Snodgrass said. "Because their boys are more than just shining representatives of this school. They are shining examples of our future.

"In this very auditorium, on the afternoon the boys set off on their trip, I called a school assembly. And I asked your children what they wanted for their futures. Of course, we all know they're young. Few of them have any idea what the future holds. But they do have dreams. And they're admirable dreams, about being doctors and activists and Web site designers and painters and professional athletes and even, bless them, teachers.

"Then I told them about Denton, Wendell, Eddie, Elijah, and Bijay. Boys who were already on the paths to their dreams. And I held up this."

From his pocket, Snodgrass produced a sheet of paper covered in lines of black circles. Eddie winced, guessing what it was.

"Scantron. No, it isn't a city in Pennsylvania. It is, unfortunately, what determines so much of our children's future. It's a test sheet. Number-two pencil. Fill in the bubbles. A, B, C, D. Sounds absolutely awful, doesn't it? Well, I held this sheet up to your children just as I am holding it up to you. And I'll be honest with you. There were more than a couple of boos coming from the audience. So what I did next was this."

Snodgrass tore the paper into little pieces. He threw it into the air like confetti.

"I told your children that the only way to beat a test is to ace that test. Show the world that you're better than the test. Dreams cannot be quantified, I told them. And I made them a promise. Perform beyond expectation on Friday's Idaho Tests, and I will put in a petition to the local, state, and federal government asking that we reconsider how we are valuing our children. I promised them I would fight to make the Idaho Tests a thing of the past.

"The reaction to this proposal was enthusiastic, to say the least. They started preparations for the greatest pep rally this school has ever seen. We'll be holding it Thursday morning, so that on Friday they are excited and motivated to conquer those tests. And what do any of us want more for our children than to see them motivated? To see them bursting with passion to be the best children they can be. To watch them achieve, and love achieving, and to know they will live lives brimming with success."

Snodgrass's voice reached a frenzied pitch.

"And our children are stepping up to that challenge! I trust you've noticed a difference in them already?"

Eddie thought about Tyler. Tyler was different, all right. A different person entirely. And the one thing Tyler couldn't stop talking about was the Idaho Tests. Eddie had endured his share of Snodgrass's lectures, and there was no way one corny speech could turn the school's delinquent into its most dedicated scholar.

"Now, I know you have a lot of questions," Snodgrass went on. "So let's open up the room, and I'll do my best to explain everything that's going on here at school."

A fidgety man stood up from the crowd. In his hand he held a crumpled wrapper, which he shook violently. Rather than waiting to be called upon, he just started speaking.

"Who exactly thought it was a good idea to hand our cafeteria over to a corporate entity? To a polluter of our bodies and our environment?"

The man then threw the wrapper onto the stage.

A smattering of applause followed.

"If you're talking about Mackers," Snodgrass said calmly, "then I have to say I understand your concerns, but you might have been misinformed. We did vote on this issue last year, and the majority of the community agreed that Mackers is a good idea for our school. And I'm not only speaking about their financial contribution. If you review the menu, you'll see the standard hamburgers and fries. But you'll also find salads and fruits and fresh-baked breads and more than enough healthy alternatives. In fact, when comparing their menu to the standard school menus approved by the FDA, you'll find Mackers is higher in daily allowances, and completely void of trans fats. This information comes not from me, but from our new resident expert, Nurse Gatling. Nurse Bloom, who served this school so well for the last few years, has decided to leave us, but in her place we have hired a registered nurse and certified nutritionist with over twenty years of experience."

Snodgrass bent over and picked the wrapper up from the stage. As he folded it and calmly placed it in his pocket, he said, "As for polluting our earth, I cannot speak on behalf of Mackers, but I do know they contribute ten percent of their profits to sustainability programs. Even Al Gore eats Mackers."

Eddie enjoyed Mackers as much as anybody, but he could hardly call it health food. The first and last time he ate Mackers before a cross-country meet, he nearly got sick in the final mile. Even after eating the salads, he felt as though he needed to shower.

Still, Snodgrass's answer silenced the man, who hung his head and returned to his seat.

"Yes, Ms. Garlan?" Snodgrass said, pointing to a hand sticking up from the crowd.

A woman in a green pantsuit rose from her seat, straightening her jacket as she stood. "You say you have such contempt for tests. But don't you think there's a place for testing in the educational system? How else are we going to measure success? I like the fact that my kids are finally turning off the TV and hitting the books. That they're obsessing over a test rather than over a computer game."

"First off, I wouldn't say I have contempt for tests," Snodgrass explained. "I just think there are other approaches to education."

"Don't you stand to benefit as well?" she continued, looking to Eddie a bit like Peter Pickle. "As I understand it, the school board is ready to appoint a new superintendent. High test scores will make them look kindly upon an administrator. And seeing that Principal Phipps has abandoned our children with his poorly timed leave of absence, I would imagine you're the next in line."

She made a good point, which hadn't occurred to Eddie in all the confusion of the last few days. What was Snodgrass going to gain from all this? How was he going to benefit from Eddie's suffering? It made Eddie sick with confusion and anger.

"Let's not get ahead of ourselves," Snodgrass said with a laugh. "I am honored by your suggestion, but the appointments of the school board are the least of my concerns. When I came to this school, the students were unmotivated, unruly, and unhappy. All I've been trying to do is show them it doesn't have to be that way. I've been trying to get them excited again. The way to do that is by showing them the importance of discipline, and by motivating them and letting them thrive in any number of ways. Sports. Theater productions. Writing workshops. Debate teams. Math clubs. These are all integral parts of an educational system. Tests have their place, but they don't make our kids unique individuals. I say we might as well just get them out of the way quickly, and focus on the important things."

The woman straightened her jacket, sniffed contemptuously, and sat.

Snodgrass pointed to another hand in the crowd. "Mrs. Haskell?"

A young woman in jeans and a T-shirt stood up. "Frankly, I'm a little worried about the kids," she said. "Motivation is great and all, but this sudden obsession with academics baffles me. What about kids being kids?"

"In the last couple days," Snodgrass said, "these kids have been as happy as I've ever seen them. They're having fun. And to illustrate that fact, we've organized a little surprise for the parents tonight. Without further ado, I present you with our newest performing troupe, singing their medley 'I Heart Ho-Ho-Kus'!"

All the lights went dark as Snodgrass stepped to the side.

Eddie suddenly felt dizzy. He wrapped his fingers around the steel bands of the catwalk and got a good grip. He imagined the whole thing crashing down from the ceiling and landing on the stage. That would be Snodgrass's true surprise—Eddie's descent, Eddie's defeat.

The thought lasted only a few moments, but it didn't seem too far-fetched. He now knew how it felt to have an enemy. And with Snodgrass in such obvious control, Eddie knew how it felt to have an enemy that was winning.

A blue light erupted from the calamity of bulbs below him. It hit the red curtains at the back of the stage and transformed them into a rich purple. A band started playing the tune to "Heigh-Ho!" from *Snow White and the Seven Dwarfs*.

The curtains opened, and seven kids dressed like the Dwarfs marched onto the stage whistling and singing:

*Ho-Ho-Kus, Ho-Ho-Kus, it isn't hocus-pocus*
*That this old town*
*Is the best around*
*Ho-Ho-Kus, Ho-Ho-Kus, Ho-Ho-Kus, Ho-Ho-Kus . . .*

Eddie groaned. This was even worse than the fall concert, which had consisted of nearly two hours of medleys of Oscar-winning songs. He was almost relieved. Maybe nothing had changed, really. School was still school.

But as he watched for a little longer, he noticed that his classmates seemed too calculating, too precise in their movements. They were whistling without missing any notes. They were *too* good.

As the kids whistled, the music slowly mutated until it took on the tune of the title song from the musical *Oklahoma!* Eddie recognized it from music class, where they had been learning all the classic Broadway hits.

Another group burst onto the stage, hooting and stomping. They were decked out as cowboys and cowgirls, but he couldn't recognize any faces. They all moved exactly the same. It was like watching a flurry of ants. And when they sang, it was in perfect harmony:

*Hooooo-Ho-Kus! Oh yes, you've quenched our thirst*
   *to roam*
*Now that we've shown we're worthy*
*To live in Jersey*
*And call this lovely place our home!*
*Hooooo-Ho-Kus! Every day we come to school in*
   *smiles!*
*If the world needs proof*
*We'll shout it from the roof*
*And they will know our name for miles!*

The audience clapped. The cowgirls skipped. The cowboys galloped. Had this been a typical school performance,

Eddie would have been tempted to crack a joke to anyone within earshot. It was, after all, a lame set of lyrics.

But there weren't any jokes surfacing in his mind. Only a feeling that he was watching something unnatural, something wrong.

The music faded softly away until all was silent. The stage went dark. Then the distinctive melody to "Amazing Grace" filled the auditorium.

As the spotlight beamed down on a tiny girl in a white dress, Eddie finally recognized someone. It was Sally Dibbs, the new girl from the Midwest. Eddie had heard her sing in music class before. She sounded like, well, a pip-squeak.

But when Sally snatched the microphone from the stand and began singing now, her voice was huge.

> *Ho-Ho-Kus, how sweet a school*
> *That taught me how to sing*
> *Within my heart,*
> *And from my mouth*
> *This song will always ring!*

The stage lights came on and Sally was joined by a swarm of kids in matching red T-shirts and blue jeans. The T-shirts were emblazoned with the slogan:

HO–HO–KUS! WHERE HOME IS HYPHENATED!

That was when he started recognizing faces. Mary Dobski. Ray Felton. Hal Melman. These weren't talented performers, like Bijay. These weren't brownnosers, like

Denton. Heck, they weren't even athletic, like Eddie. These were the type of students who went to school because they had to, who spent more afternoons in detention than at extracurricular activities.

A blast of music roared forth. It was the tune to "God Bless America." Everyone onstage began a synchronized dance routine, and they sang in haunting harmony, their voices getting louder with every line:

*We love Ho-Ho-Kus*
*Celebrates our goals*
*We believe her, never leave her*
*'Cause she's kind to our minds and our souls*
*From Waldwick, down to Ridgewood*
*To the parkway—thick with cars*
*We love Ho-Ho-Kus*
*It's written in the stars*
*Weeee . . . loooove . . . Ho-Ho-Kus*
*This humble school of ours!*

As the song reached its climax, the kids linked hands and made a heart formation. They danced at an astounding speed. In the middle of the heart, a smaller group of kids started tossing each other into the air.

What would have been a spectacular cheerleading stunt was rendered even more stunning by the impeccable timing. In the flashing lights and pounding music, kids flipped and twirled and were caught and tossed right back into the air until the whole thing resembled a fireworks display.

*Weeee . . . loooove . . . Ho-Ho-Kus*
*This humble school of ours!*

Every kid was utterly possessed, and the audience was utterly entranced. It was simultaneously the nerdiest, creepiest, and most wondrous thing Eddie had ever seen. As the audience exploded into applause, he felt a chill grip his body so tightly he feared it might never let him go.

# Chapter 16
# BIJAY

From his bunk, Bijay watched Wendell work away on the computer. He was slowly rocking back and forth as he typed, almost as if he were keeping a rhythm. If I ever play a computer programmer, Bijay thought, I'll make sure to do the same.

"I think Eddie's back," Wendell said.

Bijay turned so that Wendell didn't realize he was being watched.

As Wendell backed away from the hole, Eddie's face appeared. He had gotten better at squeezing through, and was quickly back in the room.

"So?" Denton asked.

"Remember our classmates? They're zombies now," Eddie said matter-of-factly. He flopped down onto a bunk and massaged his scalp.

"The flesh-eating type?" Bijay asked, his mind awash with images of a decrepit horde, arms out, rigid-kneed, moving slow. Just like in the movies.

"Not really," Eddie said. "They were talented. Organized. They did the most incredible song-and-dance routine. People loved it."

"Not exactly what one thinks of as zombies, Edward," Denton said.

Eddie sprung up from the bunk and gestured wildly as he spoke. "I know, I know, but their eyes. They were all like . . . brainwashed. Remember Tyler? Exactly the same. I don't know what's happening, but kids are changing."

He then began explaining the PTA meeting in detail. Bijay was jealous to have missed it. It sounded like the finest show the school had ever put on.

"So, what you're telling us," Denton said, crossing his arms, "is that everyone in our school has turned into dancing zombies, and everyone else is thrilled by this?"

"I don't know if people are thrilled," Eddie said. "But apparently kids are doing better in school. Heck, they're even having a pep rally on Thursday, they're so excited about the stupid Idaho Tests. Parents go nuts for that sort of thing."

"What about *our* parents?" Wendell asked.

"They were there," Eddie said. "And they looked good. It seems like they may actually believe we're in Canada. Or at least they're pretending to."

"Makes sense to me," Elijah said, wiping his glasses on his *MacGyver* T-shirt. "Think about it. Idaho Tests coming up. Snodgrass tightens the screws. He tricks the cool kids, or blackmails or bribes them, and makes them straighten up. The rest of the kids follow like sheep."

"Peer pressure? Trust me, this is a lot more than peer pressure," Eddie said. "If you saw it, you'd understand."

"Did you see Nurse Bloom?" Wendell asked.

"You can forget about Nurse Bloom," Eddie said. "Snodgrass made an announcement. She's gone."

"What?" Wendell said, standing up.

"She abandoned us," Eddie said. "Or Snodgrass got to her. Who knows? She's just gone. She failed."

Wendell took two steps forward and in one swift motion, he punched Eddie square in the nose. The shot sent him rocketing against the wall and onto the floor.

"Don't ever say that about her!" Wendell's voice was half bark and half whimper. "She did what she could. She's doing what she can. She never fails."

Bijay froze. When Eddie pulled himself up, Denton and Elijah went to his side.

"Eddie?" Denton said with concern. Then he placed his hand on Eddie's shoulder.

Wendell climbed into one of the bunks and rolled over to face the wall.

"I'm fine. I'm fine," Eddie said, rubbing his face.

But Bijay wasn't fine. He started to feel sick to his

stomach. He hated what he had just seen. He hated what he had just heard. And he hated a thought that was invading his mind.

"What exactly is going on with Mackers?"

Bijay remembered the first time he ever tasted Mackers. He had arrived at Newark International Airport on a flight that originated in Delhi, India. He was five years old and had flown the entire way by himself.

A flight attendant accompanied him through the terminal until they were greeted by his cousin, a smiling young man named Vikram. The attendant gave Bijay a loving pat on the head and handed him his backpack, which was filled with photographs of his parents.

"Best of luck," she said.

"We are the lucky ones," Vikram said, shaking his tiny hand. "We have the honor of welcoming Bijay to our home."

Bijay forced a smile.

"Grandfather and Grandmother will be in India for a little longer than expected," Vikram explained. "Just a few more of your parents' things to take care of, so you'll be staying with me until they get back. You are okay with this?"

Bijay nodded. He didn't really have a choice.

As Vikram led the way out of the airport, Bijay walked slowly, taking in as much as he could. He wasn't exactly scared of his new home, but it was certainly overwhelming. The India he knew was a crowded and busy place, but there was a different sort of energy to America. It wasn't that there were more people. There weren't. There were just more lights.

And the biggest light of all was Peter Pickle, a glowing neon statue mounted on a metal rod and spinning above the entrance to the food court's Mackers. Bijay stopped and stared at it, captured by its gentle motion.

"Ah, Mackers," Vikram said. "But they have Mackers in India now too, right?"

Bijay nodded.

"You've never actually eaten it, though, have you?"

Bijay shook his head.

"Well," Vikram said, "this may be your last chance for a little while. Grandfather and Grandmother do not serve beef in their house. They are good Hindus. Your parents were Hindus too, correct?"

Bijay shrugged his shoulders.

"Did they eat beef?"

Bijay shook his head.

"Well, I do. In America, people say you have the freedom to do what you like. And you, my little friend, should let me know if you'd like to eat some Mackers. It won't offend me if you don't." Vikram smiled.

Bijay didn't need to hear anything else. He led the way into the restaurant, straight to the counter, where Vikram ordered him a Burger Buddy Meal with a hamburger, a fruit cup, and a Peter Pickle finger puppet.

It wasn't necessarily love at first bite. But after chomping down on his first Mackers hamburger, Bijay really wanted another taste. He wanted to sit in that booth forever, to eat and eat and not think about all the new things that were waiting for him outside.

As he ate the hamburger, each bite became more and more familiar. Before he knew it, the hamburger was gone, and while he wasn't really hungry anymore, he probably could have eaten another three.

"Good, right?" Vikram said.

"The best," Bijay said, the first words he spoke in America.

Eight years and hundreds of burgers later, the thought of Mackers was now leaving a bad taste in Bijay's mouth. Something sinister was afoot.

"Seriously, guys." Bijay sighed. "Have you thought about Mackers?"

"We have an assault here and you're yapping about hamburgers?" Denton said.

"No, really, think about it," Bijay said. "Mackers started serving food on Monday. That's when kids started changing. Remember what Eddie said about the cafeteria? Mackers, the Idaho Tests, it all fits together."

"Sounds a bit science fiction," Denton said. "If—"

Before he could say another word, there was a deep rumble in the walls. The growl was back.

"And what does that sound like?" Bijay said, suddenly defensive. "Sounds a bit horror to me."

Denton gulped. Then he nodded, conceding the point.

Bijay wasn't happy about it. Mackers was like a friend to him. He'd defend its name to anyone. He'd sneak it into his house at night, and when his grandparents were sleeping, he would scarf down the burgers as he watched movies on his laptop. He trusted Mackers. He trusted that it would always be the same no matter where he bought it, when he ate it, or how he was feeling.

Now his school was changing, and Mackers was at the heart of it. Bijay wondered how he could ever have been so gullible. He found himself panting heavily, his lungs trying to keep up with his pounding heart. He leaned against the wall.

"We all need to calm down," Eddie said. It was the last thing Bijay expected to hear from Eddie. "Did he, um . . ." Eddie pointed to Wendell, who was still curled up on the bed. "Get the computer going?"

Wendell didn't move or make a sound.

"We need a user name and password," Denton explained. "Useless without them."

"Don't computer guys just type away and then the screen fills up with a bunch of flashing letters and numbers and then, kabam!" Elijah said. "You're in the system."

"That's what someone would do in a Bourne movie," Bijay lamented.

"This isn't a movie. This is real life," Denton said.

*Real life?* Real life is being imprisoned in your school? Real life is your classmates acting like zombies? It was feeling less like real life to Bijay with every moment. He was surprised that there weren't hidden cameras watching their every move. He was surprised Jacob Wade wasn't out quoting everything they said.

Wait a second, he thought. Of course.

"It *is* a movie," he said excitedly. "It's all a movie."

"I wish it were," Elijah grumbled.

"No, really. There's proof that we're innocent!" Bijay shouted. "There's proof about Mackers, about Snodgrass, about everything. We just have to go out and get it!"

# Chapter 17

# WENDELL

The others huddled in the corner of the room and spoke in hurried whispers while Wendell remained on the bunk. His exile was self-imposed. Still, he doubted they wanted him involved in their scheming. He couldn't believe he had hit Eddie. His rage had come on so quickly; he hardly realized what he was doing. And it wasn't exactly something he could take back.

Useless—that was Denton's assessment of Wendell's computer. Essentially, he was right. Without a user name and password, it *was* useless. Wendell's work had been for nothing, and as the others discussed their plan, he knew it was best just to stay out of their way. His skills had been tested, and proven to be failures.

As Wendell lay there, he caught just a few words: *Jacob Wade. DVDs. Locker. Cheerleaders. Flour. Wendell.*

He could only imagine what they were saying about him. He plugged his ears with little bits of paper and faded off to sleep.


On Wednesday morning, McKenzie entered the room with bloodshot eyes.

"Morning. Morning. Rise and shine," he said, forcing the words out.

Wendell scanned the room. For now, everything was well hidden. There was nothing to spark McKenzie's suspicion.

McKenzie set down the morning's breakfast. "Everyone is holdin' up?" he asked.

"Yes, sir," Denton said.

Then the coach pulled up a chair. He let out a grunt as he eased his large body onto the seat. Wendell could sympathize.

"Two more days," McKenzie said. "That was the deal, right?"

"According to Snodgrass," Elijah said.

"Let me tell you something about deals," McKenzie said. "The only deal you should make is the one to be true to what you believe. Break that deal, and you find yourself . . . well . . ."

"What are you saying?" Denton asked.

"I'm just talking," McKenzie said, rubbing his eyes.

"Eat up, guys. Stay strong. You're doing well. I'm so . . . I'm . . . Eat up."

Then McKenzie pulled himself to his feet. He gave them a toothless smile. As he pushed the door open, he sighed. At least, that was how it sounded to Wendell.

"I didn't like that one bit," Elijah said. "Something's changed. I don't think he plans to let us out. We really have to get out of here."

"Easier said than done," Denton said. "Tomorrow's the pep rally and the day after that is the Idaho Tests. To stop whatever Snodgrass is doing, we'd have to do it before then, and we still haven't figured out how to open any of the doors."

"Could Eddie do it all alone?" Bijay said.

"I'm fast," Eddie said. "I'm not magic."

Wendell listened to them from the bunk. They were capable guys, and he was sure that whatever they had spent all night planning was clever enough. But they were still in way over their heads. Magic was probably about all that would help them.

From his pocket, Wendell pulled out a pencil and the tattered Sudoku puzzle. He wished he had a whole book of them. After he finished this one, what else could he do to pass the time?

He started plugging in numbers—a three here, an eight there. Wendell had gotten to the point that he rarely made mistakes, yet he found himself stumped. It wasn't working. He looked at the top of the puzzle.

Solutions to our problems? True heroes employ patience. Every puzzle requires abilities life leaves you.

He started over: a nine here, a two there, a six . . .

It still wasn't working. Even the puzzle that Nurse Bloom had given him was useless. She had let him down in every possible way.

He read over the strange message again. It was written in looping cursive, as elegant as the nurse herself. He ran his finger over the ink. Then he stopped.

He felt excitement bubbling up inside him. It was the same feeling he got when doing an equation. There was always a solution. Always a path to the end. Sometimes he just had to start over and look at things differently.

"Stop the pep rally!" he yelled.

He sat up and banged his head against the bunk. It didn't stop him. He thrust the Sudoku puzzle in the air and shook it.

"She didn't abandon us," he continued. "She left us a code."

"What are you talking about?" Denton said.

"The message. It's an acronym," Wendell said. "Nurse Bloom slipped it past Snodgrass. See what she wrote: *Solutions to our problems? True heroes employ patience. Every puzzle requires abilities life leaves you.* Take the first letter of each word and you get *Stop the Pep Rally!*"

Denton's eyes narrowed for a second. "Okay?" he said. "That's wonderful. But it doesn't help us."

"It helps when you have the combinations to the doors!"

"What?" Denton said.

"This isn't a Sudoku puzzle," Wendell explained. "In Sudoku, you line up all the numbers one through nine in all the lines, and you put the numbers one through nine in all the boxes. You can't duplicate any of the numbers in any of the lines or boxes. Obviously, you have to be given some numbers as a starting point."

"So? Seems easy enough," Denton said.

Wendell rolled his eyes. "You see, on this one, on Bloom's puzzle, the starting point numbers she gave me don't work. The puzzle can't be solved."

"So she's not a puzzle master."

"But they'll work as combinations for the doors!" Wendell shouted.

"How can you be so sure of that?" Denton asked.

"Because when she gave it to me, she told me, 'Open it when you're ready,' " Wendell said. "She didn't mean the envelope. She meant the door. She said she'd get us out of here. And Nurse Bloom kept her word!"

"And she wants us to stop the pep rally?" Denton asked.

"That's what it says." Wendell smiled.

"Which is a coincidence," Elijah said. " 'Cause we were thinking the same thing."

"We should tell Wendell the plan," Bijay stated with a firm nod. "Perhaps he can help."

This was the first thing Wendell had liked the sound of in a while. There was just one issue. He looked at Eddie sheepishly.

Eddie shrugged his shoulders. "Whatever," he said. "If he can help."

"I might be able to," Wendell said.

"In theater club," Bijay started explaining, "Mr. Gainsbourg always tells us to play to our strengths. . . ."

● ● ●

156

As Bijay described it, the plan was simple enough. Denton was to be the talker, the charmer. Wendell would serve as the technician. Eddie's speed and agility would once again be put to the test. Elijah was going to write a rousing speech. And Bijay had to act. He had to pretend.

They spent the entire day working out the details, and in the evening, they sent Eddie out for supplies. Wendell wasn't sure any of it would work. But it was better than any game he could ever play. And he was starting to realize that sitting in that room and waiting things out wasn't going to solve anything.

He had to have faith—in the guys, and in himself.

# Chapter 18

# DENTON

It was early on Thursday morning. Denton sat on the edge of his bunk. He stood up and walked quietly to the door. Looking back, he could just barely see Wendell's hair poking out from the edge of his blanket. He turned away and lifted up the small device that Coach McKenzie had given them nearly a week before. Press the red button, an alarm will sound, and McKenzie will come running—that was what they'd been told.

He clenched his teeth and pressed the button. Nothing happened at first, and he worried it might not be working. He looked nervously at the bunks.

"Come on, come on," Denton whispered, looking back and forth.

Then he heard the footsteps down the stairs. He hurried to the door and leaned against it.

As the door swung back, Denton swung with it, falling into the arms of a bleary-eyed Coach McKenzie.

"What in the . . . ," McKenzie grumbled.

"Shh!" Denton said hurriedly. "We can't wake them. We can't allow them to know that we're keen to their mutiny."

"Mutiny?" McKenzie said, pushing Denton up and peering through the darkness to the bunks, where sounds of light snoring crept up from the frozen lumps beneath the blankets.

"An insurgence," Denton whispered. "You can't imagine what they have planned. Give me some privacy and I'll tell you everything."

"Kensington," McKenzie said, "don't think I'm about to let you out. Step aside and I'll get to the bottom of it."

"But they're traitors, Coach. And they want to escape and stop the pep rally. They've got this place booby-trapped like a pharaoh's tomb. I'm lucky I'm not strung up in a net as it is."

McKenzie looked to the ceiling, where a series of bed-sheets dangled in some elaborate contraption. Then he pulled Denton out to the landing and shut the door.

"Speak," McKenzie said forcefully.

Denton managed to keep his cool, even though it seemed the coach was about to explode.

"You walk through that door and you'll be hanging by

your ankles in less than a second. They were up all night setting a trap for you. And it really works. They tested it."

"Is that so?" McKenzie said.

"I'm afraid it is," Denton said plainly. "The plan was to trap you, and all five of us were going to walk out the door."

McKenzie stared at Denton. He motioned to him to sit on a small plastic chair that was set in the corner, then stood in front of him, hands on hips.

"And you tell me this . . . why?" McKenzie said.

"Because I hate them," Denton said, a bead of sweat surfacing on his forehead. "They don't listen to me. They're like everyone else. They tease me. And I'm fed up with it."

"So what do you want me to do?"

"Nothing. I just wanted to stop them from getting through the door. I don't want them to succeed."

From behind the door, the sound of a buzzer went off. It lasted a few seconds and then went silent. It was followed by low, mumbling voices.

"They're awake," Denton said.

"And you're gone," McKenzie said. "What are they gonna think of that?"

"Honestly, I don't care," Denton said. "Heck, if you want to hand me over to Snodgrass, go ahead. I'm just hoping those guys are scared right now. After all the mischief they've been up to, they deserve it. They don't respect authority. They don't follow instructions. They have no concept of the importance of wisdom."

"Is that so?" McKenzie said, taking a seat on one of the

steps leading down to the landing. There would be no sneaking past him—he blocked the entire stairwell.

Denton looked across the landing at him. "What do you expect from a gang of dweebs?"

The coach eyed him suspiciously. "They're good guys, you know," he said.

"Excuse me?"

"You've spent six days in there with them," McKenzie said. "And you still can't see that?"

"I see where I am right now," Denton said. "And it's exactly where I need to be."

# Chapter 19
# WENDELL

The light from the desk lamp in Snodgrass's office reflected nicely off Wendell's bald head, redirecting itself to the darkened window. The sun would be up soon; Wendell had to work fast. He carefully sprinkled flour on the computer keyboard, just a light dusting that was barely noticeable in the dark.

He ran his hand over his head. It was so weird to feel stubble where his hair used to be.

Wendell stood up and walked across Snodgrass's office. He opened the door to the closet and stepped inside. As he pulled the door shut, he stepped into a bowl of water. A bowl of water? A dog's bowl?

• • •

Only one hour before, he had been back in the room sitting in a chair.

"Why do we have to shave my head again?" Wendell had asked Bijay, who was standing behind him with hair clippers poised.

"If we glue your hair to the fake heads, then it will be more convincing," Elijah explained as he stuffed lumps of clothes under some blankets. He then placed a volleyball wrapped in papier-mâché on a pillow. Wendell could see that in the dark, the setup might pass for a group of sleeping boys.

"And combined with the tapes of snoring, the alarm clock, and the debate club you connected to the timer," Bijay went on, "it should be enough to trick McKenzie."

"Then it's up to me," Denton said, his voice wavering more than Wendell had ever heard. "I just have to chat him up for, what . . . three hours?"

"You'll do fine," Elijah said confidently.

There was a sound at the door. As it swung open, they all stopped. Eddie emerged from the darkness on the other side. Stepping into the room, he held the Sudoku puzzle in the air and said, "Open sesame! The codes work. Every single door, even Snodgrass's office. Thanks to Nurse Bloom, we're in business."

Now in the closet in Snodgrass's office, shaking water off his foot, Wendell was where he needed to be.

"In position," he whispered into the microphone he had rigged up to a homemade headset.

"In position," he heard Bijay's voice echo back. Then he heard Eddie say the same thing, and then Elijah.

They were ready.

Wendell waited in the silence for a few minutes, until he heard footsteps in the hall and someone opening the door to the office.

The sun was now coming up, and there was enough light angling through the window and a big enough crack in the closet door for Wendell to watch Snodgrass slink to his desk.

"The snake is in the grass," Wendell whispered into his microphone.

Snodgrass carried himself like a man who had total control. Like a man of purpose, a man of confidence. A foolish man, for he did exactly what Wendell wanted him to do. He sat down at his computer and typed in his user name and password. The screen lit up, displaying his desktop wallpaper—an absurd photo of Snodgrass with his thumb at his chin as if he were contemplating the deepest of thoughts.

Wendell tapped his microphone three times, the signal.

Not more than a second later, there was a rattling noise in the hall.

Eddie.

Snodgrass stopped, stood, and walked cautiously to the door. He craned his neck around and into the hall. Wendell knew it would be empty, and Eddie would be hidden up in the ceiling, shaking a maraca he had borrowed from the music room.

When the sound came again, it was farther down the hall, but loud enough that Snodgrass stepped out of the office.

Perfect.

Quietly, Wendell emerged from the closet and headed straight to the computer. He set his watch down next to the keyboard and turned on its light. The flour he had sprinkled on the keys glowed. He could easily see Snodgrass's fingerprints.

He grabbed a pen off the desk and wrote the letters on his hand: *E R O A S D G L X N*.

Then Wendell blew lightly across the keyboard, sending the flour into the air like pollen. He snatched up his watch and backed into the closet. He knew Snodgrass would return at any moment.

His prediction was right. Snodgrass stepped into the office, a look of annoyance on his face. "Lousy old pipes," he grumbled.

He hurried to his desk, where he sat down, lifted up the phone, and dialed a number.

"Hello, sir. . . . Yes, it's me again. . . . Tomorrow, day of reckoning. . . . Yes, sir. . . . You have my guarantee. . . . We shall see, oh, we shall see. . . . What can I say, other bidders, others with uses for it. . . . Understood, and it's one of many generous offers. . . . And to you as well."

He placed the phone down, smiling to himself. Then he hunched over his computer.

Through a crack in the closet door, Wendell tried to see what was on Snodgrass's computer screen. He had no idea what kind of wickedness the vice principal could be up to. Was he e-mailing his coconspirators at Mackers? Or plotting more evil to unleash on Ho-Ho-Kus Junior High? Or covering his tracks, framing more people, disguising what actually happened to Nurse Bloom?

After what seemed like an eternity of silence, a cackle like machine-gun fire suddenly burst from Snodgrass. He doubled over in his chair.

"Priceless," Snodgrass said between his hideous giggles. "Xerxes has got to see this one!"

Over Snodgrass's curled back, Wendell could finally spy the computer screen. A short video was playing on a loop, over and over again. It started with a small cat sitting in front of a short fence. The cat eyed it for a moment, then jumped. But he didn't quite clear the fence. His stomach struck the edge of it, sending him into a flip and landing him on his back on the other side. It was an uncharacteristically clumsy move for a feline, and had made Wendell laugh the first time he saw it. But that was two years ago, and he hadn't laughed nearly as hard as Snodgrass.

"Stupid stinkin' cat!" Snodgrass bellowed, spinning around in his chair like a child. He gave a high-pitched, satisfied sigh and said, "Oh, Xerxes will love it!"

Then Snodgrass was on his feet. He hurried to the door, and before Wendell could figure out what exactly was happening, the door was closing.

"The snake is slithering. The snake is slithering," Wendell said into his microphone. "Is it almost time?"

"Almost there," Eddie's voice came back.

"Someone's here," Elijah said, a clanging sound in the background, then a crash.

"Elijah?" Wendell said. There was no response.

The only other thing Wendell could hear was muffled talking. He figured Bijay must have placed the microphone in his pocket. Bijay was out of contact too.

It did no good to worry about the others. He looked at

the letters written on his hand: *E R O A S D G L X N*. He could use them to spell *Snodgrass*. Then he was left with *E*, *L*, and *X*.

"What's Snodgrass's first name?" Wendell said into the microphone.

Eddie was the only one to respond. "Nurse Bloom called him Lionel."

Of course! It was all so simple.

Wendell burst through the closet door. He was still alone in the office, but this was a big risk—Snodgrass could return at any moment. That darn user name and password had been haunting Wendell for the last couple of days. He couldn't pass up this opportunity.

He hefted himself into Snodgrass's chair and pulled up to the computer. The screen was blank except for the security panel. He typed slowly, careful not to make any mistakes.

```
USER NAME: LSNODGRASS
PASSWORD: XERXES
Welcome to Ho-Ho-Net! Administrator
     access granted.
```

The first bell of the day rang out. Homeroom would be starting in a few minutes.

# Chapter 20
# ELIJAH

Elijah stood in front of a mirror in the girls' locker room. He wet his fingers in the sink and then ran them through his hair. It always surprised him how long his hair could get when it was wet. His dripping bangs hung down as far as his chin. He wiped his wet hands over the large *H* on the polyester shirt he had just pulled on.

He had been there for what seemed like hours when he sensed something moving through the room. My imagination, he thought. I'm just tense.

Though he couldn't help wondering if the growling beast was close by. He couldn't help but worry that Coach

McKenzie had sniffed out Denton's ruse, and was now back in the gym searching for him. From his pocket, he pulled out the speech he had written. He whispered the words to himself. By this point, he had it memorized, but the repetition set him at ease.

A series of metallic clangs invaded the darkness. It sounded as though someone was running their hand across the locks and locker doors. And there was nothing imaginary about it.

Elijah stood up from the bench and walked backward slowly. When he reached the wall, he slid along with his shoulders pressed against it until he was in the darkest corner of the room.

"Someone's here," Elijah whispered into his microphone.

Before he could make out who it was, a person came running at him and slammed him up against the lockers. His earbud popped out of his ear and the microphone fell to the floor. Two eyes locked onto his. He was now nose to nose with Tyler Kelly.

Neither of them said a word to each other until the first bell rang out.

"Hey, old buddy," Tyler said. "You're gonna be late for homeroom."

Tyler's breath stank. His hair was a mess. His eyes were bloodshot.

"Uhhh . . ."

"Jeez, JK Scowling," Tyler said. "I thought you'd be happy to see your pal Tyler."

Elijah gulped and responded, "Just surprised is all."

Tyler took a deep breath, and it almost looked as if he

was going to cry. Then his voice suddenly got serious. "What's happening to me?" he said.

"I'm not sure I know what you mean."

Tyler eased his grip on Elijah's shirt. "There was a room," he said. "And you guys were asking me questions. I wasn't really thinking about what I was saying. The words were just coming out."

"Yeah?" Elijah said.

"And when I got home and went to bed, there was something I just couldn't get out of my brain. We were friends, you and me. You know, back when we were kids."

"We still are kids," Elijah corrected him.

"You know what I mean," Tyler said. "Anyway, I was thinking about our prank phone calls. And I was remembering all the crazy stuff I've done. And I started to feel a bit bad about it all. Now I always feel a bit bad about it all. But on Monday, I hadn't felt bad, I hadn't felt good. I hadn't felt anything all day. I hadn't felt real. You get me?"

"I think so," Elijah said softly.

"I realized I needed to feel real. So the next morning, I forced myself to remember more things. And the more I remembered, the more I realized that something was wrong. So I've been skipping school. I've been hanging out in the woods behind the football field during the day. Principal Phipps hid his car back there, and I've been just sitting in it. Whenever my head starts feeling less real, I just get in the backseat and try to remember things until . . . it gets real again."

"Phipps's car is in the woods?"

"Listen!" Tyler snapped. "I'm not finished. My head is still all over the place. And everyone in school is acting crazy. But you seem fine. All I want you to do is tell me if I'm going to feel, you know, completely real again."

"Have you been eating Mackers?" Elijah asked.

"Not for days," Tyler said. "I really want to, though."

"You're stronger than most. It's the Mackers that's doing it," Elijah said. "And I bet you'll keep feeling better if you stay away from that garbage."

"You think?"

"I hope."

It was at that moment that Elijah remembered when he had met Tyler. It was on the first day of the first grade. They had been sitting at the same lunch table. They didn't say much to each other as they ate, but Elijah remembered the look on Tyler's face. It was best described as devastated.

"What's the matter?" Elijah had asked.

"I had ice cream money," Tyler had whispered. "But I accidentally threw it out with my lunch bag."

Elijah had reached into his pocket and pulled out four quarters. He had slid them across the table to Tyler, and the next thing he knew they were friends.

Tyler had that same devastated look on his face right now. It clung there for a moment, then fell away as he finally looked Elijah up and down. "You're dressed like a girl," he said. "Why are you dressed like a girl?"

"Because I'm . . . we're . . . going to make things how they were," Elijah said confidently.

"Sure thing, sweetheart," Tyler said. "Let me ask you this, though. Do you know how I came to school this morning?"

"No idea."

"You will, Eliza. All of them will." Tyler took a step back, winked, then gave Elijah a gentle shove against the lockers.

"Oh, there they are," Tyler said, looking down and reaching into a trash can in the corner and pulling out a handful of papers. "Right where the note said they would be."

He looked at the papers in his hand. His eyes lit up. Elijah could see the bully in him returning. It wasn't pleasant, but it was genuine.

As Tyler walked back into the darkness, the sound of a fire alarm echoed through the locker room.

# Chapter 21
# BIJAY

The smell of Mackers permeated the school. Bijay struggled to ignore it, trying not to breathe through his nose. He tucked his headset into his pocket and stepped into the mass of students that were making their way through the halls to their lockers.

The students surrounding him were orderly, though not as robotic as he had expected. They were chatty and purposeful, moving along like an undefeated sports team accustomed to effortless victory. The girls were staid and proper, their hair pulled back into tight buns. The boys had perfectly tousled hair and wore dark jeans and button-down shirts.

Bijay had paid attention to how Tyler was dressed a few days before and tried his best to reproduce the look. His wardrobe consisted of one of Elijah's T-shirts, a faded vintage acquirement that proclaimed BAN THE BOMB. Over that, he sported one of Denton's shirts, unbuttoned, with the sleeves rolled up. He wore his own jeans, because they were the only ones that would fit his funnel-shaped bottom half. His hair was combed into a haphazard part. He had a messenger bag slung over his shoulder.

For Bijay, it was the performance of a lifetime, because he was doing something he had never been able to do: he was fitting in. Eddie had instructed him on how the kids in the auditorium moved, which he described as part swagger, part march.

As Bijay stood among his transformed classmates, he took in all the subtle details—the unblinking eyes; the stiff fingers; the crisp, flat lips—and adjusted his body and his expression. He improvised until he was just one of the many.

But he couldn't waste any time. He scanned the hall. There was one person he needed to find: Jacob Wade.

When Bijay had first joined the AV club, Jacob had been the president, and Bijay had admired his flawless movie memory. In time, though, he'd grown weary of Jacob's unsettling habits. As much as he hated to think badly of anyone, Bijay had to accept the truth about Jacob: he was an annoying slob.

Burps served as punctuation at the end of Jacob's sentences. He put mustard on just about everything he ate. Mustard was always crusted on the corners of his lips and the cuffs of his shirt. He carried a tattered backpack that was stuffed with used napkins, half-eaten tacos, and a pair of plastic nunchakus, which he would invariably pull out in the locker room and swing around clumsily as he quoted kung fu movies.

And oh yes, the movie quotes. He never stopped with the quotes.

The Jacob Wade Bijay spotted at the end of the hall didn't look anything like he remembered. He was now a dashing young man in a blue jacket and a perfectly weathered, suitably ironic yellow Bon Jovi T-shirt. His hair was swept back in an artful wave.

As Bijay shuffled through the crowd, he was met with sideways glances from each student he passed. He had to be careful not to arouse suspicion, but he also needed to focus on Jacob.

The stress of the situation started to work its way into Bijay. He took a deep breath of air, and the aroma of Mackers invaded his body. He winced as his stomach lurched. Sweat began blooming on his brow as he caught up to Jacob.

"Bijay, lovely to see you," Jacob, said, turning around. "My goodness. Are you ill?"

"Oh, heavens no," Bijay said, battling to keep his composure. "Not ill at all. Just a tad tired."

"The tired are the weak," Jacob said, his voice emotionless. "The weak have no place. Remember, my friend— success does not take naps."

Bijay nodded and gathered himself. He readopted the cold expression of his classmates and spoke in a polite, steady tone.

"Jacob. Do you remember in AV club? You told me you secretly made copies of all the school's security videos. You said that you were going to post them on the Internet and use them as blackmail. You said you kept them—"

"In my locker," Jacob confirmed. "Yes, I said and did a lot of stupid things back then. Obsessing over entertainment— what rubbish. Those days are over."

Bijay's heart stopped. That was exactly what he didn't want to hear. "Did you . . . get rid of the old ones?" he asked carefully.

Jacob shrugged. "Who has time for spring cleaning? We have Idaho Tests to worry about."

"Right," Bijay said, letting out a sigh of relief.

"We should quiz each other," Jacob proposed as they made their way down the hall. "See who's more prepared."

"We need to get our books, though, correct?" Bijay asked.

"We'll walk and talk," Jacob said. "Don't tell me you're incapable of multitasking?"

As much as Jacob had annoyed Bijay in the past, at least he had been unique. Now he was frighteningly lifeless and just plain rude. He started firing questions at Bijay as if they were programmed into him.

"Pop quiz! In what year did the First Continental Congress meet?" Jacob said.

"Ummm . . . 1776?"

"How about 1774?" Jacob said sharply. "Okay, redeem yourself. Name one of the presidents of the First Continental Congress."

"Ummm . . . Thomas Jefferson . . . no, no. Alexander Hamilton. Definitely Hamilton," Bijay said firmly.

"Try Peyton Randolph. How about Henry Middleton?" Jacob said, shaking his head. "You're in dire straits, my friend."

"I suppose I am," Bijay said.

The sound of lockers opening and shutting was an almost perfect piece of percussion. The school was simply pulsing with energy. And before he knew it, Bijay was standing with Jacob right next to his locker.

Bijay looked up at the ceiling, then down to the floor. It was a long way between.

"Bijay?" Jacob asked as he opened up his locker. "How come you're such a failure? I thought you were in Mensa or something."

"I was told the same thing," Bijay said.

Inside Jacob's locker, Bijay spied a carefully stacked pile of DVDs, each meticulously labeled with a date and location. Failure? This was a success! On these discs, there had to be evidence of Snodgrass framing them, of Mackers altering the school's food. He froze for a moment, marveling at his good fortune.

"A locker, Bijay," Jacob said condescendingly. "For books and such. I suggest you scurry off to yours."

Jacob proceeded to swing the door closed, but Bijay broke out of his daze. He caught the door before it could latch shut.

"Dweeb!" he hollered.

"Pardon?" Jacob said, clearly annoyed.

"I'm a . . . dweeb!" Bijay yelled.

"No argument there," Jacob said.

Just as the words slipped out of Jacob's mouth, a white dust rained down onto his shoulders. He moved to brush it away, and a rumbling sound came from above. Not thunder. Something different.

As Jacob looked up, the rain of dust became a rain of ceiling chunks, the foamy remnants of a flimsy drop panel. And landing in the middle of the hallway was Eddie, wearing nothing but running shoes and white underwear.

"Morning, Mackers fans!" Eddie said, standing on top of the broken ceiling panel and flicking a salute to the crowd. "I'd love to chat with y'all. But I've got a deficit of attention and a hankerin' for mischief."

He flashed them a thumbs-up; then he began running. It was Eddie at his wildest and purest and Bijay wanted to laugh with delight, but he needed to stay on course. As Eddie tore around the corner, giggling madly, Bijay took his chance. He lunged for Jacob's locker. Jacob was too busy assembling with the others, trying to figure out what was going on, to notice him.

While Bijay stuffed his bag full of DVDs, he looked over his shoulder and watched as Jacob coolly walked to the wall and, following the school's emergency protocol, pulled the fire alarm.

As the alarm blared, Bijay zipped up his bag and walked in the opposite direction of the crowd.

In the audiovisual lab, Bijay piled dozens of tiny discs on the table. He scanned the labels. "East Wing—April 12," "Back Hall—April 7," "Main Entrance—April 10," and so on and so forth.

Then he began dividing the discs by location and date. He figured he'd watch them in fast-forward and then zero in on the moment when Snodgrass orchestrated their framing, when he planted the money in their lockers. Then he'd scan the discs from the school's kitchen. Hopefully, there would be evidence of Mackers tampering with the food, adding something to the burgers and fries to brainwash the student body.

Bijay would edit the footage together and, if he had time, add a little sinister music to the sound track. Finally, assuming Wendell had done his job of disabling all the school's security systems, he'd broadcast it on all the monitors in school. This included the digital projector in the gymnasium, which would turn the wall into a veritable movie screen. Elijah would take it from there, delivering a speech at the pep rally that would put everything in context.

It was a long shot, for sure. But it was the plan.

He popped the first disc—"Snodgrass Office—April 12"—into the player. As Bijay pressed Play, he took a deep breath through his nose . . . and he stopped.

His nose didn't lie. The Mackers smell was everywhere in the school, but now it was thicker than before. It was unmistakable and unavoidable. If he was going to concentrate, he needed to do something about that smell.

Hounding around the room, he located the source of the scent. It sat on an empty shelf, upon its unfurled wrapper, as if it had been laid out especially for him—a Double Double Triple.

What a glorious culinary week it must have been at school! Mackers for every meal. Gazing at the burger, Bijay was consumed with equal amounts of longing and jealousy.

He picked it up, held it to his nose, and drew in another big breath. His hand began to shake. Surely one bite wouldn't hurt?

No, he thought. I'll just smell it. That will get rid of the urge.

Of course, it was a silly idea. Inhaling the vapors only made him want it more. So he considered just touching it with his tongue. Not swallowing, just tasting. The taste could linger on his tongue and that would be all he needed.

But before his mouth could reach the roll of the burger, he bit down hard on his tongue to remind himself how serious this was.

He carried the burger across the room, all the way to a window. With one hand he pulled down on the black shade, then shot it spinning skyward. The room was splashed with daylight. With his free hand, he pried open the window. Spring air spilled in, his first fresh breath in a week. It was time to end this.

With a sidearm fling, Bijay chucked the burger outside. It landed in the parking lot, where it bounced once like a hunk of rubber, then split open, spilling its innards onto the concrete.

There was a sink next to the window, a deep-basined model that was once used for developing photographs. Bijay turned the tap on, and splashed cold water onto his warm face.

Then he held his mouth under the stream and started gulping the water down. It tasted clean and pure. It tasted like victory.

He wiped off his mouth and hustled back to the video

monitors. As he pulled his headset from his pocket, he looked closely at the communication device Wendell had built for him, an ingenious contraption of tiny wires, speakers, and microphones.

Instinctively, he cracked it open. Then he grabbed a stereo cord from a box at his feet. He used it to plug Wendell's device into a sound board, and adjusted the sound levels.

He smiled to himself. Why hadn't he thought of this before?

The sound board lit up. Voices began babbling forth from a set of speakers.

He pressed Record.

# Chapter 22

# DENTON

When the fire alarm rang out, it blared so loud that it felt like shivers through Denton's body. He had been sitting with Coach McKenzie on the dark landing outside the room for almost two hours. They hadn't said much to each other. McKenzie seemed perfectly content with sitting there in silence.

Denton looked up at the ceiling with concern. After about thirty seconds, the alarm stopped.

McKenzie nodded to him knowingly. "The others—they're fully prepared, right?"

"Pardon?"

"Don't pretend I'm a fool," McKenzie said. "That's Snodgrass's job. I know more than I let on."

Denton gulped. McKenzie just grinned.

"Europeans talk about their long history. Do you know what that room is?" McKenzie said.

"It's a bloody, god-awful prison."

"I guess you could call it that," McKenzie said. "But it hasn't always been. It was built, the foundation of it anyway, over three hundred years ago. How 'bout that? Back then, it was a root cellar, a place to keep vegetables. I think the guy was a Brit, an immigrant like you. Made his wealth and the root cellar soon became a wine cellar, with a mansion dropped on top of it. In the eighteen fifties, it was a stop on the Underground Railroad. Hundred years later, the cold war had begun, and it was reinforced and turned into a bomb shelter. State bought the land and built a school here in the sixties. The mansion was converted to a series of classrooms, but the bomb shelter remained. Cold war ended in the eighties. They closed that room up, took down the reinforcements, ran pipes through, and it became a memory of past times. Snodgrass decided it should serve another function."

"How do you know all this?" Denton asked.

"When I was your age, I went to this school," McKenzie said. "I wrote a report on this room. It was an important thing to know about. Snodgrass thinks it's a place to hold people. This is a museum, boy. A piece of history. A place to teach people."

What's going on here? Denton thought. I'm enjoying listening to Coach McKenzie. He isn't yelling at me. He's actually being interesting.

"I've been *this* many places in my life," McKenzie confessed, holding up three fingers. "New Jersey, where I was born. Louisiana, but only for basic training. And South Korea, one year along the Demilitarized Zone. A world away. I haven't been to war. I haven't seen much. Good gravy, would I like to see more. England, maybe. Bharata's from India, right? Gotta be quite a place. But for now, my heart and my duty bind me to this little piece of earth. And I'd like to think it's just as special as anywhere else."

"There's a map in your office. It's got thumbtacks all over it. What's that, then? Your allies? Coalition of the willing?" Denton said condescendingly.

McKenzie chuckled. "The red ones are places I've been. The green ones are places I'd like to go."

"A lot of green ones."

"A lot of places," McKenzie said plainly. "A lot of money to get to them."

McKenzie paused. Then he reached into the pouch of his sweatshirt and pulled out a wad of money.

"What's that?" Denton asked.

"What I'm worth," McKenzie said. "You deserve to know."

"That's a lot of money."

"Not really. It's what we took from your lockers. And what Snodgrass promised me for doing this job."

"Bake-sale money?" Denton asked.

McKenzie shrugged. "It's amazing what you can convince yourself to do if you think you're acting in everyone's interests."

"Are you trying to make me think you were helping us?"

"No," McKenzie said. "I was punishing you. But I was

also sparing you shame. And I was helping you take your punishment like men."

"And you still honestly think we deserved it?" Denton asked.

"Honestly . . . does it matter?" McKenzie said. "There are bigger concerns now. I keep my ear to the wall. All is not right with this school. Growling in the walls. Snodgrass spittin' all over Principal Phipps's legacy. I followed my orders and my orders were wrong."

"It's the Mackers," Denton said. "That's what's changing everything."

McKenzie looked puzzled.

"Really?" he said. "I've been eating the Mackers all week. There was one thing Snodgrass told me, though. . . ."

McKenzie's voice trailed off as he stood up. Denton hardly recognized the man standing above him. McKenzie puffed up his chest. He took off his Marines cap and placed it on Denton's head.

"You've done an admirable job, Kensington," McKenzie said. "Let's go round up the other guys. I know they're not in the room. So where are they really? This might be worse than I thought."

# Chapter 23
# WENDELL

**A**lmost as soon as he disabled the fire alarm, Wendell heard Snodgrass's voice at the door to the office.

"Settle down, Xerxes."

A phlegmy cough accompanied it. It sounded like it came from a troll.

Wendell quickly logged off the computer and rose from the desk. When he began to turn around, he noticed something.

His butt was still stuck in the chair.

His size had played yet another sick joke on him. Wendell, destructor of chairs, was now connected to one.

He tried desperately to pry it off, but there was no time.

"Crap, crap, crap . . . ," he said under his breath as he swiveled back and forth, trying to figure out what to do.

Snodgrass was entering the code to the door. Wendell had no other choice. He backed into the closet, the chair protruding behind him and knocking things from the shelves.

The office door swung open just as Wendell made it safely into the closet. He put his hand over his mouth to shield the sound of his heavy breaths. Claws clicked on the tile floor. There was a metallic squeak like a rusty gate. And then the sound of a snorting nose running across the bottom edge of the closet door. Wendell closed his eyes.

"SOS," he whispered through his fingers into his microphone. "The snake is in the grass. . . . The snake is in the grass. . . ."

"My chair is missing, Xerx?" Snodgrass said. "Why is my chair missing?"

Wendell watched as Snodgrass circled around his desk and picked up the microphone for the PA system. Lifting it to his mouth, he pressed the button.

"Good morning, Ho-Ho-Kus Junior High. I trust everyone is having a lovely start to the day. It has been brought to my attention that there was a disturbance this morning in the east wing. Nothing to worry about, children. Everything is under control. But in lieu of our first-period classes, we are going to start our pep rally a little early. Cheerleaders, please assemble in the locker room. Band members, in the gymnasium. Everyone else, report to home-room, and your teachers will lead you from there. Failure to report to the pep rally is . . . a failure. That is all."

Snodgrass placed the microphone down and stalked around his office, looking for his chair. "Where is it, Xerx?" he said.

Wendell could still hear the slobbers and snorts at the bottom of the door. He prayed that someone had heard his distress call.

"You don't want that water, Xerx," Snodgrass said. "Let's get rid of it."

Snodgrass approached the closet door and grabbed the handle.

"Hey, Snod-nose!" came the sound of a familiar voice.

Snodgrass swung around. "Mr. Green," he said with a sneer. "To what do I owe the honor?"

Wendell peered through the crack to see Eddie standing in the doorway. He was dressed in nothing but white underwear.

"I'm just showing that I don't hold grudges," Eddie said with a smile. And even though he was talking to Snodgrass, Wendell was pretty sure the words were really addressed to him.

"Isn't that nice," Snodgrass said, stepping toward Eddie. "Glad to see you back upstairs. Though I don't think your attire is exactly up to our dress code."

"We both know I've never been up to code," Eddie said.

"Xerxes," Snodgrass said softly. "Would you please do something painful to that boy."

Claws clacked across the floor, there was a low growl, and a dark shadow moved away from the closet.

Wendell smiled to himself. He had always thought of Eddie as brazen and reckless. His recklessness had now saved Wendell. It was also keeping the plan on track.

"And they're off," Eddie said, standing in a runner's stance. And then he *was* off. Wendell could hear Snodgrass and Xerxes bolting out after him and shutting the door behind them.

Wendell lifted his microphone up. "Thank you, Eddie."

"No. Thank you," Eddie panted back. "Now finish the job."

Wendell hurried to the computer. His final task was to establish a link between the AV room and the projector in the gym. The rest would be up to Bijay and Elijah. Wendell only hoped they were okay.

First, he had to work at extricating himself from the seat. His butt was still lodged between the two arms, and it would take a significant amount of wiggling to remedy the situation.

As he was trying to use the wall to pry the chair off, there came a knock on the door. He paused. Snodgrass wouldn't knock, would he?

"Hello," Wendell said cautiously.

"Wen?"

He knew the voice. In a flash, he was rolling in the chair across the room, his legs scrambling like crab claws.

When he opened the door, it was like opening the gateway to his dreams. Because there she stood, gorgeous and graceful, her face full of empathy.

"Oh, Wen," Nurse Bloom said. "We gotta get you outta here."

# Chapter 24

# EDDIE

Eddie had been going for a few minutes, leading Xerxes in circles and curlicues and trying to ignore the strange feeling in his ankle. But it was getting worse.

As he rounded yet another corner, the numbness shifted and the ankle began to throb. The juice of adrenaline was wearing off. His leg buckled.

Eddie had never been injured, at least not seriously, but now his ankle was swelling up. Crashing through a ceiling onto a hard tile floor can do that. His pace slowed. On the wall behind him, there was a giant shadow that looked like a lion, or maybe a gargoyle.

A snarling, gurgling sound accompanied the shadow. It was getting louder by the second.

The pain radiated up Eddie's leg into his back until his leg quit completely, and he collapsed onto the floor.

He had to keep moving. Eddie dragged himself along with his hands like an injured soldier from a battlefield. He watched as the shadow grew even bigger.

Then he finally saw it: Xerxes.

The shadow was deceptive, to say the least. Xerxes wasn't much bigger than a loaf of bread. And more than half his weight was concentrated in his round, snub-nosed head.

His shriveled back legs were bound together and held off the ground in a sling. A pair of wheels extended from his hindquarters, as if he were a Roman chariot. Xerxes galloped down the hall toward Eddie, kicking off from his front legs and riding the momentum on the two squeaky wheels.

If this was a dog, it was the ugliest dog Eddie had ever seen. It was a saliva-slinging, mutant bobblehead on wheels. And within seconds, it was launching itself onto him.

He quickly stuffed his microphone and earpiece into the waistband of his underwear, rolled over, and used his hands to protect his face from Xerxes' assault. It consisted of the beast gnawing on Eddie's neck and making strange guttural noises, a gurgling *robble, robble, robble*.

Snodgrass rounded the corner, striding with confidence. He clasped his hands together in delight.

"Oh, Xerx." He laughed. "You caught your first delinquent!"

"Get him off me!" Eddie cried, less concerned about the damage Xerxes was inflicting than the embarrassment of being caught by a dog on wheels.

As Snodgrass drew closer, he said, "Oh, Mr. Green. This must be so disappointing for you. You must have thought you were so clever."

"Cleverer than this little monster," Eddie said.

"Xerxes? Why, he's a prize Chuggle. Part Chihuahua, part pug, part poodle. Superior breeding."

Snodgrass was soon standing over Eddie. He bent over and scooped Xerxes up in one arm. He kissed him lovingly on the cheek, though the dog kept wiggling and slobbering.

"Attaboy, Xerx," he said.

"You've got me," Eddie said defiantly as he rolled over. "So what?"

"I've got you," Snodgrass hissed. "But I'm far from done with you."

With one hand on the back of Eddie's neck, Snodgrass guided him down the steps to the room. There was no telling how this would play out. In a moment, they'd be face to face with McKenzie and Denton, and the plan would be officially exposed.

Snodgrass gave Eddie a shove. "Move it," he said.

Eddie limped his way down through the darkness. When they reached the landing, there was nobody there.

"Where's McKenzie?" Snodgrass said.

Eddie had no answer. Eddie's job was to distract Snodgrass, while Denton's job was to distract McKenzie.

Maybe the plan was completely falling apart. Eddie only hoped that Elijah and Bijay were finding more success.

As he punched the code into the door, Snodgrass muttered, "It doesn't matter where he is, this will all be over soon."

"What do you mean?"

"I mean," Snodgrass said, opening the door, "you, him, none of this will be much use to me after tomorrow."

"Because of the Idaho Tests?" Eddie asked. "Everyone will ace 'em and you'll be made superintendent? That's the plan, right?"

"The plan, Mr. Green," Snodgrass said with a laugh, "is not nearly that stupid."

He flicked the lights on as he poked his head through the door. Sheets hung haphazardly from pipes attached to the ceiling. Fake heads made out of papier-mâché poked out from beneath blankets on the bunks. The debate-club recording continued its drone.

In the dark, the setup might have fooled McKenzie. In the light, it was fooling no one. Snodgrass pushed Eddie inside.

"Owww," he groaned, his ankle throbbing. In any other situation, he would have been making a run for it. The pain was just too much, though.

"Get over it," Snodgrass said, stepping inside. He eased Xerxes to the floor, and the dog immediately went into hound mode, sniffing around the room.

Snodgrass walked over to the bunks and started pulling all the sheets and blankets away, sending the fake bodies tumbling to the floor.

"Pathetic little charade." Snodgrass tossed a sheet to Eddie. "Cover yourself, Green. You're an embarrassment."

Eddie begrudgingly obliged, wrapping the sheet around his body like a toga. Xerxes tugged at the corner of it.

"So, where are the rest of the dweebs?" Snodgrass said.

"Beats me."

"Doesn't really worry me," Snodgrass said as he tied two thin blankets together. "We'll wrangle them up."

"Who? You and your genius army?"

"The students, you mean?" Snodgrass chuckled. "Remarkable, aren't they? Fact is, I'm almost finished with them as well. You think this is all about a silly test, don't you?"

"It isn't?" Eddie rolled his eyes. Snodgrass had to be lying. If it wasn't about the test, then what could it be about?

"The test is just the last thing to put on my resume," Snodgrass explained as he tied the end of one of the blankets into a lasso. "You really believe I want to be dealing with zit-faced losers the rest of my life? A bigger future awaits a man who can control the masses. I've been fielding offers."

"From who?" Eddie was starting to feel out of his league. He couldn't picture Snodgrass as anything *but* a vice principal. Then again, he didn't really know how adults thought.

"Whoever pays," Snodgrass answered. "Corporations. Governments. Bring on the highest bidder."

Then Snodgrass twirled his blanket-lasso in the air and

tossed it over Eddie's head. It fell around his body and landed on the floor at his feet.

"Uh . . . ," Eddie said.

The next things happened in such quick succession that Eddie could do nothing to stop them.

Snodgrass threw the other end of the lasso over a pipe and gave it a yank. The hoop of the lasso tightened around Eddie's ankles. Then Snodgrass put all his weight into it, slamming Eddie into the floor. Like a captain hoisting a sail, Snodgrass hoisted Eddie in his snare.

Three seconds later, Eddie was hanging helplessly upside down.

"And the race is over." Snodgrass laughed. "Look at 'im, Xerx. Strung up like a rabbit."

Eddie swayed gently back and forth, his ankle throbbing and blood rushing into his head while the ceiling seemed to rumble above them.

# Chapter 25
# ELIJAH

"**. . . C**heerleaders, please assemble in the locker room. Band members, in the gymnasium. Everyone else, report to homeroom, and your homeroom teachers will lead you from there. Failure to report to the pep rally is . . . a failure. That is all."

Snodgrass's voice filled the dark locker room, sending Elijah to his feet. Suddenly it was his moment to act. Tyler was gone.

After a few minutes, Elijah heard high-pitched chatter in the hall. It seemed as though it was getting closer. He didn't care who it was. Instinctively, he hurried to the wall and started yanking at the locker doors. When he finally found one that wasn't locked, he threw it open and squeezed inside.

"By my calculations, we will have at least one thousand two hundred fifty-six people in the gymnasium," a girl said.

"Our cheers should be at least one hundred decibels, then. For optimum effect," another girl replied.

Through slits in the locker door, he saw the room fill up with green and blue, the school's official colors.

"Come on, ladies, line it up and look sharp!" someone said loudly. "A flawless performance will mean a flawless future."

They fell into two lines with ease.

"Ten minutes! Concentrate! Focus!" It was Karen Esposito calling the shots. Elijah could just see her face, as stern a face as he had ever seen.

The girls quieted down. No one said a word. For nearly ten minutes, they didn't do a thing.

Finally, the sound of an air horn leaked into the locker room from the gym.

"That's us, ladies!" Karen yelled. "Let's move! Let's motivate! Let's do this!"

They began their march out of the locker room. As soon as the last two girls were almost out of view, Elijah opened up the locker and quietly hurried after them.

The gymnasium was bursting at the seams. Students and teachers sat shoulder to shoulder on the bleachers, but everyone was calm and spoke in controlled whispers.

Elijah could see the school band on the bottom row. Their uniforms had been modified—the sleeves removed and the shoulders heightened and trimmed to sharp points. They resembled a punk-rock army created by a corporation. Which is to say, they weren't punk rock at all. Everything controversial about them was manufactured.

The lights went out, and everyone stopped talking. The band took it as their cue.

The bass drum thumped, slowly at first, then gradually faster until it sounded like a heartbeat. The band members began pumping their fists; the crowd followed suit. Then the trombones kicked in, playing a frenzied fight song.

A strobe light started flickering and the band swung into full gear. Horns were blaring. A guitar screamed. Kids were ripping into the percussion.

Elijah watched over the shoulders of the other cheerleaders, from the darkness on the edge of the locker room. No one noticed he was behind them.

Karen, standing at the front of the two lines, held up her hand and began counting down on her fingers. When she reached one, she stepped into the flashing lights of the gym. The other girls followed at her heels.

As the music slipped into a sultry beat, they sashayed to the middle of the gym, where the strobe light made them look like machines. Elijah followed a few steps behind.

With his awkward stride and his short dark hair tied into tiny pigtails, he was certainly the black sheep of the bunch. No surprise, really. It was the first time Elijah had ever held pom-poms, or worn a skirt, or stood in the middle of a gym in front of his entire school pretending to be a girl.

"A . . . B . . . A, B, C, D, A . . . B . . . A, B, C, D, A!" the cheerleaders chanted, punctuating each letter with perfectly executed kicks and pom-pom pumps.

It was impossible for Elijah to keep up. He gave it his best shot, but he felt like a dancing bear—a beastly, clumsy center of attention.

The crowd was taking notice, and rather than laughing, they were pointing and whispering. They seemed annoyed that someone was tainting a perfectly good pep rally. Elijah could feel their angry gaze, and he knew he had to just go for it.

"This . . . is . . . a . . . test," Karen chanted into a megaphone, "but it's not only a test!"

"Not only a test!" the other cheerleaders echoed.

"This . . . is . . . a . . . test . . . but it's not only a test!"

"Not only a test!"

Elijah sidled his way over to Karen. As she turned her back, he made his move, snatching the megaphone from her hand.

She froze. The other cheerleaders froze. The strobe light went off. A spotlight came on. Every eye in the gym zeroed in on the boy dressed as a girl, standing center court and holding a megaphone.

It came violently and instinctively, like a gasp for breath taken after an underwater swim.

*"Listen to me!"* Elijah screamed into the megaphone. *"You must listen to me!"*

No one in the gym made a peep. Their attention was locked on him.

The blood rushing into Elijah's head was creating a sensation of both pure fear and pure excitement. The entire school *was* listening. This was the moment he had always yearned for, the chance to incite the crowd.

"That's right," Elijah said into the megaphone, his voice cracking. "Because this concerns all of you. All of us. Do you know where I've been the last week?"

No one responded.

"Of course you don't. And you could never guess, so I'll just tell you. I was locked in a room in the basement of this school, compliments of our good friend Vice Principal Snodgrass. Why? Because apparently, I stole money from a bake sale. Hid it in my locker. Like a fool.

"It's not true, of course. But honestly, you're probably thinking what does that have to do with me? Why should I care? You should care because Snodgrass believes something that I don't think any of us believes. He believes kids like us can be manipulated. He thinks we're not capable of making our own decisions, so he makes them for us. Behold the evidence.

"Roll it, Bijay!" he yelled, pointing to the bare brick wall where the video projector was aimed.

Nothing happened. Maybe Bijay hadn't heard him. So he yelled it again.

"Roll it, Bijay."

Nothing. All eyes moved at once from the wall back to Elijah. He knew their patience was waning.

"Wendell? Bijay?" he whispered into his microphone.

Dead air.

In a room packed to the rafters, Elijah suddenly felt like the loneliest kid in the world. He scanned the crowd for a friendly face. But all he saw was a sea of conformity. For the last year, he had been writing in his journal, referring to his classmates as sheep, as carbon copies of one another, as worthless clones. It wasn't until that moment that he truly could appreciate how diverse and interesting they all had once been.

He had prepared and practiced his speech. It was supposed to be complemented by incontrovertible evidence—the images of Snodgrass's dastardly deeds.

But the images weren't coming. And as scared as he was of what might happen next, he had to just say something. The speech wouldn't work now, but maybe if he just told them what he was feeling . . . words and ideas, even in this day and age, might still be enough.

So he said into the megaphone, "I never liked any of you . . . and it's been that way for a while."

Blank stares were the crowd's response. He paused, cleared his throat, and soldiered on.

"I never liked how you dressed, how you talked, what you valued. I never liked how you treated me. You all scared me. But what's happening to you now is so much scarier. You've changed. Not because you wanted to. But because Snodgrass thought he knew what was best for you.

"Now, I don't claim to know what's best for you. But I do know you haven't been given the chance to figure that out for yourselves. You deserve that chance. Otherwise, you might as well be locked away in a room somewhere.

"When I was given that chance, I decided I didn't like any of you. That was a mistake. But mistakes aren't forever. And now when I make new mistakes, I don't want to do it alone. I want friends. Heck, I want enemies. I want to find out who all of you are, and not miss out on things. And we can all at least share that. Otherwise, if we're perfect, if we all have everything . . . we're sharing nothing. We're being no one. We're not real."

The crowd still didn't move. Elijah let his emotions loose.

"So put down the Mackers! Tell the school you're sick of perfection! Boycott the Idaho Tests and let the fear take hold! Let's do things . . . that kids are just supposed to do!"

He took a deep breath. That was it. He had said his piece. He might not have changed any minds, but at least he could walk out of there knowing he had tried.

Whispers passed back and forth through the crowd and progressed to a low murmur. Then Karen Esposito pointed at him.

"The ugly cheerleader is right," she yelled.

"Thank you!" Elijah cried, throwing his hands in the air and stepping toward the bleachers. "Finally!"

"You're welcome," Karen yelled back. "Because you are spot-on. You never liked us! And you still don't!"

"Uhhh . . ." Elijah took a step back.

"You're standing smack-dab in the path of our success, and that is unacceptable! My proposition? We clobber him!"

All at once, everyone in the crowd nodded. And all at once, they stood up. They looked like a pack of blood-thirsty penguins, equal parts creepy and ridiculous. And they were ready to attack.

"Destruction to distractions!" Karen Esposito yelled.

The rest of the gym echoed, "Destruction to distractions!"

As the kids descended from their seats, all the teachers, glassy-eyed and silent, stepped out of their way. They seemed to condone what was about to happen. Perhaps they had no other choice, Elijah thought. He closed his eyes. He had never been good at picturing his own future. He certainly hadn't pictured his end coming at the hands of a mob of overachievers. He imagined the newspaper headlines:

### DEATH BY PEP
### CHEER SILENCED BY THE TEST-OBSESSED
### OUT-DWEEBED

"Destruction to distractions! Destruction to distractions!" they chanted.

Lost in what he believed would be his final thoughts, he hardly noticed the sound of the revving motor. As the sound got louder, he opened his eyes.

The crowd had stopped advancing. Their attention had shifted to the door. That was when a bright purple minibike came hurtling into the gym. And riding it was none other than Tyler Kelly.

He barreled through the crowd, engine screaming and wheels smoking. Kids scattered to get out of his way, and those who weren't quite quick enough were pushed to the ground by their classmates.

As Tyler sped toward center court, he kicked out the back tire and did a stuntman-quality skid, stopping inches away from Elijah.

"Glad to see me?" Tyler said.

"Never thought it was possible," Elijah said. "But yes. Definitely yes."

"Settle down, Geekspeare," Tyler said, standing up. "I've got enough cheerleaders crushin' on me. I'll take care of this and be on my way."

Tyler reached into his pocket and removed a crumpled pile of papers.

"What's that?" Elijah asked.

"Gold," Tyler said. "Solid."

"Step aside," someone yelled from the crowd. "Some of us are serious students. Some of us want to succeed."

"Well, I've got some serious success right here in my hand," Tyler said, shaking the papers in the air.

"What is it?" someone else yelled.

"What else?" Tyler smiled. "The answers to this year's Idaho Tests. Want 'em? Come and get 'em."

"What are you doing, Tyler?" Elijah asked, now worried for both their safety.

"Being real," Tyler said with a devilish, knowing smile. "I was told this would help turn things back to the way they were. And isn't that what both of us want?"

Before anyone could touch him, Tyler stuffed the papers back into his pocket and, hunching over his minibike, gunned it through the crowd.

Madness followed. No one cared about Elijah anymore: the test answers were all that mattered. They pushed each other, tore at each other's hair, kicked, bit, and generally did unscholarly things.

The bleachers couldn't handle such chaos. The wood started splintering and cracking. As if fighting their way out of a crashing wave, kids and teachers rolled and tumbled from the rickety structure until they found the shoreline of the gymnasium floor. Then they were on their feet, at dead sprints.

Within just a few moments, the gym was empty except for Elijah. Broken wood littered the floor, a basketball hoop had crashed to the ground, and pom-poms lay scattered like giant carnations left over after a dance. There was a gaping hole where the supports to the bleachers once stood.

Dust flurried through the air. Stunned, Elijah stood motionless at center court. Then he heard that familiar sound, that almost forgotten growl.

# Chapter 26

## EDDIE

"I'd appreciate a thank-you," Snodgrass said.

Eddie's fingers brushed the floor and his face was sports-car red. It was difficult to speak, but he coughed out the words "I'd never thank you."

"Well, you should," Snodgrass said. " 'Cause you and your pals are going to be famous."

"Yeah, for stopping you," Eddie said. Hanging upside down, he could only see Snodgrass's feet and that nasty little Xerxes slobbering around the room.

"Wishful thinking," Snodgrass snapped back. "No, we're talking about the DWEEB serum. Proof that genetics can be manipulated by the simple act of swallowing."

"What are you saying?"

"Why do you think I kept you down here?" Snodgrass said.

" 'Cause you knew we were dangerous," Eddie said.

"You're about as dangerous as dandelions, kid." Snodgrass laughed. "No, I needed to keep your DNA pure. As the DWEEB serum was revised and adjusted, it was important to have all five of you well fed, well studied, and well . . . contained."

"You called it the DWEEB serum?"

"Of course I did. 'Cause they're you, Mr. Green. All those kids up there. Perfect distillations of you, and Wendell, and Denton, and Bijay, and Elijah. It was quite clever, actually. Get five of the brightest kids in various disciplines, throw their DNA into a blender, mix up a potion. Get that potion into the school and you have yourself a bunch of superstudents. Heck, you can even make a man act like a beast with the stuff. When I first tested this out last week, I used Xerxes' DNA. I gave it to a test subject and he—well, I'll spare you some science talk that might scramble your brain and turn you into a whirling dervish."

"My middle-school brain is clear enough to know you're insane," Eddie said, energy and anger now coursing through his body. "And that what you've done is criminal and despicable."

"What's criminal about making better students?" Snodgrass said. "What's despicable about creating a world where everyone is equal?"

"How could you possibly think you were going to get away with this?" Eddie asked.

"The same way anyone gets away with anything," he said. "Cash a check. Walk away. You may be seeing DWEEB behind the prescription counter soon. But you certainly won't be seeing much of me. Bloom and McKenzie can take the heat. And you, well, like I said, you can thank me. I've made you famous. The first *E* in DWEEB."

With that, Snodgrass gave Eddie a push that sent him swinging, then moved toward the door, snickering.

As Eddie swooped back and forth over the floor, he caught a glimpse of Xerxes chewing on one of the test books. An idea came to him in a flash. It was his last hope.

Grabbing at one of Xerxes' wheels, Eddie swiped him off the floor and sent the beast into a slobbering, wiggling rage.

"I'm guessing you'll want to take your friend with you," he said.

Snodgrass's tone became very serious. "Yes, I believe I will. So kindly hand him back before I do more than just swing you on that line."

"Go and get him!" Eddie snarled, and with all his energy he hurled Xerxes at the wall. He didn't want to hurt the dog, and luckily, his aim was true.

As Xerxes struck the Perseverance poster, it crumpled around him and he fell through the hole.

"Xerxes, oh, sweet Xerx," Snodgrass cried, running to the hole.

The pain in Eddie's ankle was nearly unbearable, but this was his chance. He clenched his stomach muscles and bent his body in half. The daily regimen of sit-ups McKenzie had forced upon them was proving most helpful. He wanted to scream but he fought the urge, gritting his teeth. Instead, he focused on grabbing hold of the blanket tied to his ankles.

"Almost got you, almost got you," Snodgrass said as he reached back behind the wall.

Snatching the blanket, Eddie tugged himself up until he could reach the pipe. He held it with one hand and untied the snare around his ankles with the other.

"Just a little closer," Snodgrass said. "Come a teensy bit closer."

Dangling from the pipe, Eddie briefly considered dropping to the floor and dashing to the stairs. His ankle couldn't handle that, though. He needed something to break his fall. He shinnied across the pipe toward the wall.

"A little closer. A little closer . . ."

As Eddie hurled himself onto Snodgrass's back and grabbed a handful of his jacket, he felt years of frustration release from his body. "Settle down, tiger!" Eddie hooted. "That's what they always say to me."

Like a rodeo bull, Snodgrass lurched back and tumbled around the room, trying to knock him off. But Eddie simply held on tight and laughed.

In a last-ditch effort to gain the upper hand, Snodgrass stopped, then shifted into reverse gear. He plowed toward the bunks.

Just as Eddie was about to be crushed against a wooden rail, he pushed off with his knees and propelled himself onto the upper bunk. And as Snodgrass's bony body jumped backward, Eddie hooked his fingers on the waist-band of the vice principal's underwear.

Everything slowed down. Eddie landed on the mattress. He yanked at the waistband and in one swift motion, he hung it on the edge of the rail.

Many kids must have had this dream, Eddie thought. But Eddie had actually done it. He had given his vice principal a hanging wedgie.

Unfortunately, he didn't have the luxury to bask in the moment. He needed to get out of there. Fast. Lowering himself off the bunk, he carefully set his good foot down and began hopping to the door.

"You filthy little brat!" Snodgrass screamed as he flailed like a fish on a line, his arms not long enough to dislodge himself, his feet dangling mere inches off the floor. It would have been nice to stay and watch him struggle for a while, but Eddie needed to find his friends.

"Hey, Snod-nose," Eddie said from the doorway. "Hang tight. I'll send someone to get you in a week."

Before Snodgrass could respond, Eddie hopped out of the room and threw the door shut.

# Chapter 27
# ELIJAH

The first thing that emerged from the chasm in the gymnasium floor was a scratched and bruised hand. Then a bald, swaying head, rising up like a cobra's, and a leg adorned with a heavy and broken chain.

Principal Phipps stood amid the rubble, gritting his teeth and shaking his leg nervously. He started biting at his own shoulder and making strange growling sounds.

"Pr-Principal—Ph-Phipps?" Elijah stuttered, not sure whether to get any closer. The man looked awful.

Phipps straightened himself up and tried to speak. "Elij—*ark!* Elij—*ark!*"

"Are you okay?" Elijah said. "Can I help you?"

"You d-d-did—help m-me. You f-found me." He hung his head and panted heavily.

"Can I get you something to drink?" Elijah really didn't know what else to say. For all the strange things he had seen in the past week, the strangest was his principal, bedraggled, beaten down, and defeated.

"No more drink!" he snapped. Then he started growling. It was the same growl Elijah had heard all week. Phipps's eyes narrowed and he started toward Elijah as if he were going to attack.

"Down, boy!" came a voice from behind him.

Phipps heeled. Elijah turned.

Eddie was hopping on one foot at the other end of the gym, wrapped in a sheet.

Phipps started twitching and making a *robble, robble, robble* noise.

"Holy cow. He's the test subject Snodgrass was talking about. He took Xerxes' DNA and used it on Phipps!" Eddie said with surprise.

"What?" Elijah said.

"I'll explain later. What happened to the others?"

"You don't know?" Elijah said.

"I don't."

"We might," came two voices.

Stepping into the gym, Denton and McKenzie resembled something impossible—a duo, a team . . . friends.

"Watch out, Denton," Eddie cried. "McKenzie is right next to you."

"Of course he is," Denton said, straightening the Marines cap on his head. "He's one of the good guys."

"Rosen," McKenzie hollered, in full gym-teacher mode. "Step aside and let's have a gander at Mr. Phipps."

McKenzie double-timed it over to Elijah and gently guided him out of the way.

"Mr. Phipps," McKenzie said calmly. "Everything in order?"

"Snodgrass . . . he poisoned . . . he turned me into . . ." He started snarling like a dog before he could finish talking. McKenzie stepped forward and placed a hand on his back.

"It's all right," he said comfortingly. "It'll be fine."

"We checked the AV room. Bijay was gone. But he set up a DVD," Denton explained. "He recorded everything everyone was saying. You won't believe some of the things we heard."

McKenzie turned to Eddie. "We got a location on Snodgrass?"

"Downstairs," Eddie said with a satisfied smile.

"I'll take care of him," McKenzie said. "You fellas track down the other two. We'll get this thing straightened out."

"He's just letting us go?" Elijah asked.

"Of course," Denton said. "He needs our help saving the school. He loves this place more than anyone."

"Get going, guys," McKenzie said, pulling a cell phone out of his pocket and flipping it open.

"Who's he calling?" Elijah asked, still shaken and confused.

"I've still got a few friends in this town," McKenzie said, leaving it at that. "Denton, remember what I told you."

"What did he tell you?" Elijah asked.

"Don't drink any water."

# Chapter 28

# WENDELL

With her soft, snowy hands, Nurse Bloom guided Wendell's chair into the parking lot. It careened from side to side, but she managed to keep it relatively straight.

Wendell did what he could, pushing off with his feet when he was at risk of toppling over. Mostly he let Nurse Bloom, her white jacket rippling behind her, do all the work. He'd happily stay stuck if it meant Bloom led the way.

"You're lucky we haven't crashed yet. I've always been a bit of a klutz," she said. "As a little girl, I used to be so afraid to do anything. In school, my biggest fear was tripping and falling into an open locker and then getting locked inside."

Wendell chuckled. In his lap, he held a large plastic bottle of water they had just filled up from the sink in her office.

"I know." She laughed. "Crazy, but these are the things you worry about. Being a kid is no fun, right?"

"I don't know," Wendell said. "It's tough, certainly."

"The kids in school now," Bloom said, "they're different . . . on another level. I would have been so jealous. Such confidence. Such drive. Impressive."

"Freaky is more like it," Wendell said.

"Yes, a bit. True. But can't you relate? You're a driven guy too, Wendell. A genius, really. Doesn't that make you feel good about yourself?"

"I don't know," he said. "It just makes me feel like . . . myself."

"And you should be proud of yourself." Bloom slowed the chair to a stop next to a solitary yellow bus, the only vehicle in the entire parking lot.

"I figured out your puzzle," Wendell said, shifting the water bottle in his lap. "The codes."

"I knew you would," she said. "I depended on it. I needed your help."

"What's the water for?" Wendell asked.

"If we're going to save the world, we'll need it," she said.

Behind them, a deep rumbling shook the school. It worried Wendell, but it made Nurse Bloom smile.

She took a step onto the bus and then reached down, grabbed the water bottle, and placed it on board. Then she descended the stairs and stepped back into the parking lot.

"Thanks, Wen," she said. She wheeled him a few yards away from the bus to a spot where they could see the front entrance to the school.

"What next?" he asked.

"I'd be willing to bet this parking lot will be full of kids any minute now."

"How do you know?"

"Let's just say I encouraged Tyler Kelly to be a little bit of bait."

"Are we going to cure them?" Wendell asked.

Nurse Bloom thought about the question for a moment. "Do you think your classmates are sick?"

"I think there's something wrong with them, yeah."

"I see," Bloom said. "When I was your age, I might have thought the same thing. And I'll admit, they have problems with their tempers, their impulsiveness, their snobbiness, their various . . . appetites. But all that comes from within you guys. And in future versions, we can weed that stuff out."

"Excuse me?"

"Imagine a world where your peers are actually your peers, where everyone can interact at the same level. Where everyone is exceptional. That's the world I wanted to live in as a little girl. That's the world we can create."

"I don't know what you're saying," Wendell said.

"When I went to Snodgrass for help," Bloom explained, "all he was thinking about was money. His greed will be his downfall. Bettering the world is what the noble concern themselves with."

Wendell looked at her burned wrists. He wondered if that was what chemical burns looked like. It was a good chance they did. Then he looked at her face. She smiled at him, and when she smiled she looked exactly as she always had—beautiful. But that didn't matter anymore. He saw deeper than that.

"I just want things back the way they were," he said.

"Really?" Nurse Bloom said. "Like when you were constantly teased? When you were in my office every day pretending to be sick? You don't want that. That was painful."

"Pain is better than being numb."

"Your naivete is adorable," Nurse Bloom said, brushing her hand across his cheek. She rubbed her knuckle against a zit that was flowering on his chin. "You know, a little medication could clear this right up."

"No, thank you," he said, turning away from her. He couldn't make eye contact.

"They'll be fine, you know," she said. "It wears off in a day or two."

"What does?"

"The DWEEB serum," Bloom said. "When they go home for the weekend, they'll go back to being boring old bullies and nobodies."

"They'll go back to being real people," Wendell said.

"Sometimes real people need improvement."

"Do you think I need improvement?" Wendell said.

"No, Wendell, you're perfect. Together with the other guys, you're everything a kid should be. Come with me. We'll make this world just like you."

At that moment, Tyler Kelly came rocketing through the front doors of the school on his motorcycle. He rumbled down the front steps and onto the concrete, his head down, one hand up, the test questions rippling in the air.

"You all suck sooo muuuuch!" he screamed gleefully.

"Charming, isn't he?" Bloom said.

Wendell watched as Tyler raced by, and as a mob of kids sprang through the doors and filled the lot.

"Now or never," Bloom said, starting to push Wendell toward the bus.

He planted his feet on the ground, putting on the brakes. "Was it always you?" he asked, heartbroken. "Was all of it you?"

"You mean the DWEEB formula?" Kids were now circling Nurse Bloom, trying to get a fix on which way Tyler had gone. "Of course. I've been working on it for years. It's simple in concept, a little harder in execution. Basically, it's just making people's DNA do impressions. Heck, we made Phipps act like a dog. But it doesn't last forever. You have to keep taking it. But with a little work, we can make it last longer. Then it won't be like impressions. People will become what we want."

"I thought it was just about the Idaho Tests," Wendell whispered in confusion.

"Oh, that was just an easy way to get Snodgrass to do the dirty work. His greed blinded him to my real plan."

"The real plan?"

"Testing it. And testing you. You had fun, didn't you? The loose cinder block. The Sudoku. The mystery. I set up quite an adventure for you. And we'll keep that adventure going. 'Cause it's going to be a rough road. People are resistant to new ideas. But with the help of my five little dweebs, we'll be unstoppable." Then she bent over and kissed Wendell on the cheek.

He wasn't sure if it was the kiss, or all the kids running around, or the fact that he was still stuck in a chair and all his blood was flowing down to his feet. But suddenly, Wendell felt dizzy.

He closed his eyes for a moment. He told himself that he wouldn't let his emotions get the best of him again. He needed to do something.

When he opened his eyes, one face among the mob stood out: Sally Dibbs.

Wendell channeled all the emotions building up inside him and focused it on the armrests of the chair. The metal bent like wet spaghetti, and he pulled himself to his feet.

"Bus to the future," Bloom said. "Leaving right now."

Wendell ignored her. He knew what he had to do. Fighting against the tide of kids, he made his way toward Sally. When he was standing in her path, he put his hand out.

"Stop!" he shouted.

She skidded to a halt. "Wendell?"

Then he said something he never expected to say. "Be annoying. Please just ask me some stupid questions."

"Pardon?" Sally said. "I will do nothing of the sort. I have to get to those test questions before everyone else does."

"No," Wendell said with confidence. "You have to be annoying. Because that's who you are. You're new, and goofy, and you talk too much, and you're not a great student, and you're a terrible singer and I used to ha— and that's who you have to be."

Sally's eyes narrowed. There was a doubtful look in her eye. She cocked her head to the side.

Wendell could see he was getting to her. He smiled widely and stood firmly in her way, and kept smiling until he heard a voice. It was a voice that used to entrance him. Now it sounded shrill and frightening.

"In here," Nurse Bloom was saying as she pointed toward the bus. "The test questions are in the back."

Kids were pouring onto the bus. Oh, this isn't good, Wendell thought. He turned away from Sally and started toward Nurse Bloom.

As more kids boarded the bus, the crowd began to thin out. And Wendell saw that there was someone holding Nurse Bloom's hand. It was Bijay.

# Chapter 29
## BIJAY

**N**urse Bloom tightened her grip on Bijay's hand. He looked up at her.

"The world, Bijay," she said. "At our fingertips."

Bijay smiled back.

"You know what?" she went on. "Snodgrass didn't think you were exceptional, didn't want you to be one of the five. I knew differently. You know why I chose you? Not because of test scores. Because you can deal with loss. You can abandon things. You know that if you play pretend long enough, you can accept whatever life throws at you."

Bijay nodded to her.

"Let him go," Wendell said, stepping toward her.

Nurse Bloom feigned a look of surprise and let go of Bijay's hand. "He's free to do whatever he likes," she said. "Right, Bijay?"

Bijay shrugged. Only one thing mattered. "I'm hungry."

"Hunger is good," Bloom said. "It keeps you alert. There's Mackers in the bus if you want it."

"Bijay," Wendell cried. "It was her the whole time. She's the one who set us up."

"I'm the one who is giving the world what it wants," Bloom said plainly. "And I'm giving Bijay what he wants. He's new and improved."

"Bijay?" Wendell said. "You didn't eat the Mackers, did you?"

Bijay shook his head, though it was hard to remember anything. All his brain kept telling him was "feed me." Memories only got in the way of the task at hand.

"It's not in the Mackers!" someone shouted.

Bijay turned. Descending the front steps were Elijah, Denton, and Eddie, who was hopping on one foot.

"It's in the water!" Denton shouted. "He must have drunk the water."

"Very perceptive," Bloom said, pointing a finger at Denton. "You guys are always one step ahead of the curve. If you all get on the bus, we can use that ingenuity to make the best strain of DWEEB possible."

"Bijay," Eddie shouted. "We caught Snodgrass. We found Phipps."

"And thanks to you, we've got everything on DVD," Elijah said. "Snodgrass's whole confession. It's over."

"It's in the water," Denton said again. "Everyone's obsessed with Mackers because Bijay is obsessed with Mackers. But if they stop drinking the water, they'll be okay."

"Don't go, Bijay," Wendell said. "She's tricking you."

Bijay understood what the four of them were saying, but it didn't matter to him. It didn't solve his hunger.

"Come on, Bijay," Bloom said, reaching out her hand. "Say goodbye."

Bijay grabbed her hand and took a step onto the bus. He looked back over his shoulder. "Good—"

"Remember something," Elijah shouted, cutting him off. "Something meaningful. Something about who you were . . . who you are. Something real."

"Say goodbye," Bloom told him again.

That was when Bijay stopped. A memory had fought its way to the surface of his mind.

He remembered walking through a tree-lined campus where his parents worked as professors. He remembered being between the two of them, holding both their hands as they waved and smiled and said thank you to everyone they saw.

He didn't realize until years later that what they were really saying was goodbye to their colleagues and students. And he didn't realize until just now, standing on the steps of the bus, that they were also helping him say goodbye. They were giving him one last look at their lives before he got on that plane to America.

His father died a few weeks later. His mother, the following week. And the day after his mother's funeral, he was eating Mackers in the airport.

From Bijay's perch on the steps of the bus, he saw a banner that hung above the entrance of the school. It read:

## Mackers is here!

His hunger receded until it was replaced by a feeling of deep loneliness. He let go of Bloom's hand.

"Bijay," she said. "The time is now. I'm going."

"I think I want to go with them," he said politely.

"That would be a mistake," Bloom cooed. "You'll see. This is just the start of so many wonderful things. Just think. Someday, everyone will be smart. Everyone will be polite. Everyone will eat what they want. Everyone will be exceptional."

"And everyone will be alone," Bijay said plainly. He stepped down and away from the bus.

Nurse Bloom scowled. Anger, something Bijay had never seen in her, now consumed her face. She threw the door to the bus closed. A few second later, the engine coughed to life.

As Bijay walked toward his friends, he concentrated hard, trying to sift through his scrambled memories.

As the bus pulled away, Eddie started after it.

"We can't let her get away," he shouted, but his limp was slowing him too much. He stopped after just a few yards.

It didn't matter.

Because that was when Bijay saw an eruption of light at the edge of the parking lot, and heard a chorus of sirens as a line of police cars, fire engines, and ambulances came into view.

All the escape routes were blocked. All the students were frozen in their tracks. The bus stopped.

Before he could figure out what was happening, men in uniforms were hurrying at Bijay. Their arms were outstretched. He couldn't understand what they were saying at first. When they were lifting him up, he heard them loud and clear.

"You're the ones. Are you okay? Get inside," they were saying.

# Chapter 30
## DWEEB

"**Y**ou have got to be kidding me," a police officer said, pacing through the tiny basement room. "The entire week?"

The boys, who were standing in a line against the wall, nodded back. Another officer looked at the hole. He stuck his head in, then pulled it back quickly. "Um, is that a dog back there?"

"You could call it that," Eddie said.

"That's Xerxes!" Snodgrass protested, his hands behind his back tugging at his underwear. On his wrists hung a shiny new pair of handcuffs, the perfect piece of jewelry for the soon-to-be-former vice principal.

"I've heard about enough from you," the first police officer said, guiding Snodgrass out of the room.

"It's amazing what these boys accomplished," Coach McKenzie said. "And I'm sorry for the trouble I caused." Then he held his wrists out to the other police officer.

"What are you doing?" Denton protested.

"What's right," McKenzie said.

"I hate to do this, Coach," the officer said, attaching the handcuffs. "But we're glad you called."

"It's nice to know your students remember you and believe you," McKenzie said.

"Coach!" Denton called as the officer led McKenzie to the door.

"Kensington?"

"Don't worry," Denton said firmly. "You'll get to see the green ones."

McKenzie smiled. "And you'll come to love New Jersey," the coach said as he exited.

A fireman stepped into the room. "Mr. Phipps is on his way to the hospital. Your parents are on the way here," he said. "There's a lot to explain. I just know they'll be glad to see you. I'll walk you to the parking lot to meet them. If you need our help telling them what happened, you have it."

As they followed the fireman back outside, they saw the parking lot was already empty. It was as if nothing had happened.

"Did you find all the kids?" Eddie asked him.

"Most of them," he said. "We've got a lot of people on it. We'll round 'em all up."

"And Nurse Bloom?" Wendell asked.

"Nurse who?"

"On the bus," Elijah clarified.

The fireman nodded. "Hold on a sec."

He walked down the steps and approached a young police officer who was standing guard at the edge of the lot. They talked for a minute or two, and then the police officer approached them, grinning.

"You were asking about that nurse?" the officer asked.

They all nodded.

"She was something else, wasn't she," he said, shaking his head. "Gorgeous, and so helpful."

"Did you arrest her?" Denton asked.

"Arrest her?" The officer laughed. "I wanted to marry her! No, she was nice enough to drive a few of the kids home in the bus. With all the craziness going on, we could use all the help we could get."

"You let her go?" Elijah gasped. "How many kids were with her?"

"I don't know. Four or five. They drove away and they were all singing like angels," the officer mused. "It was quite a sight. But not as extraordinary a sight as you guys. What are you, a bunch of superheroes or something?"

They stood five abreast on the steps. Eddie, wrapped in his sheet. Wendell, standing tall, his bald head shining in the sun. Denton, his hands on his hips, with the Marines cap perched on his head proclaiming Semper Fi. Elijah, dusty and bruised, decked out in the school colors . . . and a cheerleading skirt. And Bijay, just being Bijay.

"No," they said in unison. "We're DWEEB."

# About the Author

**AARON STARMER** studied English at Drew University, earned his master's degree in cinema studies from New York University, and received an entirely different kind of education working for ten years as a bookseller and an African safari specialist. His writing has appeared in guidebooks and a variety of humor publications, including the McSweeney's anthology *Mountain Dance Moves*. *DWEEB* is his first novel. He lives with his wife in Hoboken, New Jersey.